RANCOUR IN RUFFEC

Catherine Patterson Mysteries

GM HALEY

No part of this book may be produced by any means, nor transmitted, nor translated into a machine language without the written permission of the author

This is a work of fiction. Names, characters, businesses, places, events and incidents are either the products of the author's imagination or used in a fictitious manner. Any resemblance to actual persons, living or dead, or actual events is purely coincidental.

BOOKS IN THIS SERIES

DANGER IN THE DEUX SEVRES

VENGEANCE IN THE VENDEE

CHICANERY IN THE CHARENTE

GRIEF IN THE GATINE

PERIL IN POITIERS

RANCOUR IN RUFFEC

CHAPTER ONE

'Have a great time!' Grinned Karl.

I waved cheerily into the camera before pushing the screen down on the laptop. For several minutes my reaction to Karl's news, news which had the potential to create major upheaval in our lives, had been to stare blankly into the middle distance with an almost numb feeling. Though gradually and with a heavy sigh, I managed to force myself to snap out of it. Making the decision that as I was going to need time to consider the implications, my plans for the foreseeable future needed to take priority. So, almost as if on autopilot, I picked up my suitcase and walked to the door. Turning to scan the room, reassuring myself that everything was locked and secure, I was suddenly overwhelmed with a sense of sadness as if I was gazing at everything for the very last time. When I finally pulled open the front door, I found Di walking briskly to greet me.

'Wasn't sure if you heard the beeps,' she responded to my surprised look before moving swiftly forward to relieve me of my case. 'Any news?'

I absently allowed her to take the case from me. 'Well the job's his if he wants it.' I heard myself say.

'Oh,' Di made no effort to hide her disappointment. 'I suppose with Aiden settled back in the UK too, you'll find it easier to make your decision then.'

I smiled weakly. 'We'll see.'

Sensing that I wasn't keen to discuss the topic, she didn't comment further.

*

The *manoir,* constructed of cream stone, making it look warm and inviting, stood at the end of a short tree lined drive. Newly painted pale grey shutters framed mullioned windows and a wide set of curved stone steps sat in the centre of the building which led up to a large front door, which due to its glossy grey finish and gleaming brass fittings, made the entrance look rather grandiose. As far as I could see, the house was surrounded on all sides by well-manicured gardens and the overall look gave me the impression that the house was well loved and cared for.

Marie advised Di to pull the car into one of the allotted bays just as a red Peugeot appeared alongside. Clambering out while the other driver did the same, I glanced curiously across intending to flash a friendly smile. Unfortunately the driver was preoccupied, intent on retrieving a fishing rod and large plastic container from the boot of his car. When he finally glanced in our direction, Marie offered a friendly *bonjour* while slamming the passenger side door. The man muttered curtly in response before taking himself off toward the back of the house.

'So I'm guessing there's a fishing lake in the grounds,' Di said glancing at Marie as she hoisted a large canvas bag over her shoulder. Marie nodded. 'Henri issued licenses for it but I think it's something Geraldine is trying to discourage now that he's gone. She doesn't like the idea of strangers wandering around her property. *Évidement*, Henri enjoyed fishing so he was happy to chat about fishy things with the other *pecheurs*.'

I caught Di's eye at Marie's comment and we exchanged a grin.

Geraldine met us at the door and greeted us warmly. Both Di and I glanced at each other in surprise on hearing her flawless spoken English. A small, slim built woman with neatly cut, short, greying blond hair, Geraldine had a keen look and lost no time in swiftly appraising us before leading us into the large foyer. I gazed around to admire the décor; teal flocked wallpaper covered the walls, and a plain teal coloured carpet runner ran the length of the hallway on top of a stone tiled floor. A series of three medium sized chandeliers hung down from the high ceiling creating an overall grand look to the entrance.

After suggesting we leave our bags in the hallway, Geraldine ushered us into a large living room which was dominated by a large stone fireplace. The heavy wooden ceiling beams and two large dusty pink velvet sofas surrounding a large square coffee table with patterned tiled top, made the room, despite its size, feel cosy and comfortable. Arranged on the table were serving plates, one of which was layered with small triangular sandwiches and a large chocolate gateau sat on another. A delicate China tea set was set out ready. Each of us took a seat on the sofa just as a short, portly woman appeared carrying a large metal teapot.

'Thank you, Collette.'

The woman set the teapot down onto a tray on an antique side table next to the sofa on which Geraldine sat. Then, with a faint smile and without ever glancing up she scurried from the room, taking care to close the door quietly.

'I thought we'd have a nice English tea,' smiled Geraldine while she moved to arrange cups and saucers then sat forward to pour tea. 'How much have you told your friends Marie dear?'

Marie looked startled. '*Eh bien*, I wasn't sure how much you wanted them to know so, nothing really.'

Marie had simply said that Geraldine needed moral support to face estranged family members who would be unhappy once they found out about receiving less than expected from Henri, her deceased husband, in his will. Of course, Marie had also lured us to a short stay with Geraldine by promising sightseeing in the area and the option to visit several markets she'd claimed were popular tourist attractions.

'When are you expecting everyone to arrive?' Asked Marie.

'Oh, most of them should be here by tomorrow, they'll probably arrive in fits and starts. I've asked Collette if she can arrange some temporary help with airing the rooms etcetera so there'll be another girl, um, Malarie, around the house.'

Di and I exchanged puzzled glances before gazing back at Marie and Geraldine expectantly. Geraldine busied herself with passing cups and saucers across the table to each of us, no doubt guessing she'd piqued our interest.

'Help yourselves to milk and sugar. Oh and of course,' she pushed the plate of sandwiches a little in our direction. 'Please also help yourselves to a bite to eat.'

There were muttered thankyous, serving plates exchanged and sandwiches taken until everyone shifted to sit more comfortably. The chatter was lighthearted to begin with; Geraldine asked Marie about her family while Di and I smiled politely here and there, offering pleasantries where appropriate. But mostly I gazed around the room as they chattered, listening vaguely to their conversation about local matters. Sitting quietly gave me the chance to enjoy the refreshments as well as appraise our host, which I was keen to do after being struck by how anglicized her pronunciation of the French language was, despite having lived in France for many years.

'So, I can presume they know nothing?' Geraldine was saying, giving Marie a forthright look.

Marie shook her head and seemed to be making an effort to avoid our gaze.

Geraldine put down her teacup and sat back in her seat. She gazed at us openly.

'I need to be rather frank with you both. I know and trust Marie and her judgement so I'll presume that what I am about to say to you will not leave this room.'

I nodded faintly, wondering what on earth all this secrecy was about.

'Of course,' muttered Di, who was looking as puzzled as me.

After a moment, Geraldine nodded, satisfied that we had agreed to her condition of silence.

'Well, first of all I need to explain some background so please bear with me. I moved to France with my first husband, Freddy, long before I met Henri, when I was very young. Freddy had a well-paid job at the embassy in France, though we had met some months earlier at a high society function in London. Anyway, we lived here in France for two or three years before we returned to London. During our marriage we had three children – adults now of course and whom you'll meet over the coming days. My daughter Anne, married to Simon, my son Billy, a confirmed bachelor and my youngest Celia, recently divorced. Celia has two children but they'll not be with her. I believe the children will be staying with Ian, her ex-husband, while she's visiting.'

Geraldine paused to take a sip of tea so both Di and I took the opportunity, after having finished our sandwiches, to manoeuvre slices of chocolate cake onto our plates. Marie, I noticed, had been nibbling her sandwich very slowly as if trying to make it last and was now holding her teacup in both hands, her eyes fixed on Geraldine's face. Waiting until Di and I were sitting back and settled once again, Geraldine continued.

'I returned to France once Freddy and I divorced because I loved it so much here and brought the children with me. They spent school holidays in England so they could spend time with their father and alas, once they reached adulthood, all three returned to live there. Couldn't wait to get back in fact.' She sighed, a rueful look on her face before continuing. 'I bought this house when I first came here with the children, so it's been a family home. Unfortunately, the cost of it and the upkeep was always a little beyond my means,' she paused, staring into the middle distance as if reminiscing, then smiled suddenly and looked at us directly once again. 'But I managed somehow and several months after I moved here with the children, I met Henri. He also had children, David and Elise, but they lived with their mother, his ex-wife, in northern France. They'll also be coming here to stay with us by the way. David's coming here alone, his wife Valda is staying at home which incidentally is in your neck of the woods Catherine, *Coulonges sur l'Autize*.' She paused and I nodded to acknowledge her words.

Geraldine continued with a sigh and a roll of her eyes. 'And Elise is arriving, hopefully without Bruno, husband number *four*.' She paused once again for dramatic effect and to give us time to digest this piece of information.

I glanced at Di to find her spellbound by the intricacies of this woman's family, whereas Marie was now frowning.

'Irene and Julien, the children I had with Henri are also coming to visit, and I believe Julien is bringing his fiancée, Genevieve. They all live in France, although Irene has only recently returned here after working for several years in England. Of course, as they are bilingual, they could live here or there I suppose, it doesn't really matter.'

Geraldine stopped again to pour tea and encourage everyone to eat and drink more. After we all agreed to another cup, Geraldine peered into the teapot. Seeing it was almost empty, she took it to the door, picked up a small bell from a side table and shook it into the hallway. The tinkling sound brought footsteps before we heard Geraldine's voice. Meanwhile, we ambushed Marie with harsh whispers.

'Is there something more to this trip than we thought?' Asked Di.

'Why is she telling us all this?' I added.

Marie looked sheepish, 'Please wait until…'

She was stopped from going further when Geraldine returned. Of course, nothing got past her. As she sat down, she said, 'I know you'll be wondering why I'm telling you all this, but I wanted to fill in some of the background to the family you'll be meeting during your time here. What you may not know is that I asked Marie to be here not just for moral support.'

Geraldine looked pointedly at me. 'I've been following what's been happening in your little part of France Catherine. Marie has also been keeping me abreast of events so I requested your presence specifically.' She turned to Di, 'and of course reinforcements won't go amiss.'

Di and I traded bemused glances.

'You see,' continued Geraldine matter of factly, and ignoring our looks, 'I think my life might be in danger.'

We both stared at Geraldine in disbelief but remained silent, waiting for her to embellish us with facts.

'I see I've startled you.' She said casually before turning to Marie with a meaningful look.

Marie, taking her cue, sat forward and cleared her throat. 'What Geraldine is trying to say is that she has asked us to visit because she believes the danger is from her own family. Her own children.'

Di gasped.

'And you want us to do what exactly?' I asked Geraldine as kindly as I could while hoping to hide my dismay.

'Well dear, I want you to tell me who exactly out of my dearest children is trying to murder me!'

This time I didn't try to hide my shock. 'And you know for a fact that one of them is?'

Geraldine frowned, seeming frustrated that we didn't immediately take what she said at face value and once again turned to Marie for support.

'The family are coming here because Geraldine has requested it as a final visit because they have been informed that Geraldine is terminally ill.'

'And,' interrupted Geraldine, 'Of course I've floated the idea of a will.'

Both Di and I looked sharply at Geraldine and immediately muttered how sorry we were, to which Geraldine waved a hand, dismissing our words. 'Please, I've come to terms with it, don't concern yourselves.' Unsure how to respond I began to wonder why someone would try to murder her if they knew she was going to die soon anyway. Geraldine guessed my thoughts.

'Yes, I can see you're probably wondering why, if they know I've got a terminal illness, anyone would want to do that and don't think I haven't wondered myself. Of course, I don't know how long I've got, could be months, could be weeks or maybe I'll last another year. So maybe they simply can't wait.'

'Geraldine's recently found her cat dead, poisoned,' added Marie. Geraldine looked uncomfortable. 'You might say as we are in a rural area sometimes this happens because some unscrupulous farmers or others are trying to get rid of certain pests from their land. However, the cat was left with a note and something scribbled on it, though I couldn't decipher what it was.'

'And because of that you think your family are threatening your life?' I asked, perplexed at how she'd come to this conclusion.

Geraldine shook her head and stared down into her teacup without responding.

'Could we have a look at the note?'

'Note?' Suddenly Geraldine looked confused. 'What about it dear?' I frowned and glanced at the others who, from their bewildered expressions, also seemed to be puzzled at Geraldine's odd reaction to my question. Unexpectedly, after a few minutes of silence, Geraldine recovered her senses.

'Oh, they sent a detective, Borné his name was, yes Inspector Borné. He interviewed me several days afterwards, but he was completely uninterested. After all it was only a cat. He didn't see it as a threat.'

'And yet you do.' I muttered sceptically.

'When you meet my children Catherine, you'll see why I'm concerned.'

'What about other people that you know. Could this, er, threat have been from them? I mean were your family, your children even here, or in the vicinity when this happened?'

Geraldine nodded slowly. 'Unfortunately yes, they were all here for my husband's funeral. After I found the cat, Jacques, Malarie's father and vet, had a look at it. He confirmed it was likely the cat had been poisoned. Of course the family denied all knowledge of knowing anything about a note when I asked them about it.'

'Did you show the note to them?' I asked trying to clarify the details.

Geraldine shook her head.

'Did Jacques do a post-mortem on the cat?' Asked Di.

Geraldine shook her head.

'And it couldn't have been someone else outside the family who killed it? Maybe a neighbour?'

Geraldine again shook her head. 'I don't believe so. The only reason the family are all coming here now is because they obeyed my request to visit. They think they have something to gain, from Henri's will, or from whatever I leave in my will.'

'Killing an animal is one thing but killing a person is something else entirely. And your own family? It's difficult to believe.' I said, voicing my reservations.

Geraldine got up and went to a large antique dresser. She opened a drawer and took out a folded piece of paper before passing it to me. In scrawled letters, clearly meant to disguise the handwriting, was a stick drawn man hanging from a noose next to a simple almost childlike drawing of a house. I turned the paper over to see what was on the other side but there was nothing.

'That was sent to me several days ago, after my family were told about my failing health.'

'Strange. So, this is a second note?' I asked.
She nodded.
'Have you shown any of them this note? Or shared your fears?' Asked Di.
'Oh no, and I'm sure they'd deny sending it anyway.'
'What about the police? Were they shown the second note?'
She snorted. 'Didn't bother telling them about it.'
'What happened to the first note?' I asked, still trying to clarify the facts.
Geraldine busied herself rearranging the plates on the table. 'Oh, that detective was so disinterested, I ended up throwing it away, um, I think.'
'I see,' I said, sharing a puzzled glance with the others and feeling that Geraldine was deliberately being vague.
'I think perhaps you're still not convinced. You might be once I give you a little more background,' said Geraldine, making us all, including Marie sit up and take notice.
'So, as I mentioned, when my family arrive, they will no doubt be expecting me to discuss a will. They will be under the impression, one which I gave them, that Henri left a will. Of course, what they don't know and will be shocked to find out is that that he had nothing to leave. David and Elise from his first marriage, will be expecting the lion's share from his estate not knowing that their mother went through everything he had years ago. A gambling habit and a sob story meant he helped her out a little too often while we were together. Of course, the children were shielded from it all. He couldn't let them believe anything less of her to protect them, so they were never told about her real nature, even when they were old enough to understand. And they'll assume, as required by French law that they have some claim on this house. But this house is mine. I bought it and it's in my

name, always has been.' She paused with just enough time for us to digest this little morsel before dropping another bombshell.
'You see Henri and I never actually married, lived as man and wife yes, called each other husband and wife but never married.'
Marie looked stunned. '*Mais non*, your wedding celebration?'
Geraldine waved a hand dismissively. 'Oh it was a big con dear, put on for friends and family, even your mother, a dear friend, wasn't aware of it.' She gave Marie a rueful look. 'That's one of my biggest regrets actually, that I didn't let her into our secret. Truth is, neither me nor Henri could stomach going through a marriage ceremony again. One marriage was enough for both of us and then as time went by, it didn't seem to matter about it being written down on a piece of paper, so we just kept it to ourselves.'
'And your children Irene and Julien, do they know?'
Geraldine shook her head. 'Not a clue. And while I'm purging myself of my past sins, I might as well tell you that Henri was not Julien's father.'
Marie gasped.
'He doesn't know of course,' continued Geraldine matter of factly. 'I suppose I should tell him some time soon. His real father's long dead now anyway so not much he can do about it.'
Geraldine was starting to sound callous and my earlier snap judgement of her as a frail, but kindly old lady was changing rapidly.
'And the other children, from your first marriage?' I asked tentatively, wondering which children had any rightful claim on Geraldine's house and funds, such as they were.
'Oh yes dear, all within wedlock, all expecting something when I go – *when* of course, that's the great unknown.'
I felt shocked. She was talking about her children as if they were all gold diggers.

'So, what is in Henri's will exactly? I mean if he didn't have anything to leave.' Ventured Di.

Geraldine looked blank for a moment. 'Oh there's no will dear although I've led them to believe there is.' She shrugged. 'Henri had nothing and left nothing.'

I frowned. Geraldine's tendency to state a fact then contradict herself was making it difficult to follow the chain of events.

Geraldine gave me a direct look. 'So you see, I'm expecting the lack of a will and the fact that Henri had nothing to leave, added to the fact that Julien is going to be told that Henri was not his father is going to cause ructions.' She chuckled gleefully. 'I couldn't do all that without feeling that I have people on my side. And of course, I also need your detecting skills.'

'But surely your children from your first marriage, Anne, Billy and Celia as well as Irene would be enough to provide any support.'

She sighed resignedly. 'Anne, Billy and Celia have never quite forgiven me for bringing them to France and away from their father, who despite his failures, doted on them. They never really got on with Henri, I think mainly because they resented him for trying to take the place of their own father and as I said before, they went back to England as soon as they were old enough.'

'So Irène then?' Interrupted Di.

Geraldine looked uncomfortable for the first time. 'To my shame, I must confess that I rather favoured Irène over her brother, unconsciously at first, but Henri once confronted me about it, and I realized it was because I saw traits in Julien which I didn't like - and reminded me of his real father. Of course, Henri believed Julien was his and I made sure he went to his death bed with that belief. So yes, Irène was, and probably still is, my favourite. Unfortunately, I managed to sour that relationship too. When I discovered her wanting to marry a man I thought completely unsuitable, I made it my business to drive them apart. I did whatever I could to discredit him, convinced that he wasn't good enough for my Irène.' She paused, a sad look on her face. 'When she found out what I'd done it was too late. The man had left the area, convinced that Irène didn't care for him and married someone else within only a month or so, on the rebound I suppose.' Geraldine sighed. 'Anyway, time passed and Irène came around, not entirely having forgiven me, but we are at least now on speaking terms.'

We all fell silent.

Geraldine's gazed around at us. 'So you see, I need all the support I can get to keep me from my own children, one of which wants to see me in the ground quicker than my illness will get me there.'

'And that is why you need someone with detecting skills,' murmured Di.

'Indeed. I want to find out who is making these threats.'

Not entirely convinced Geraldine's life was in danger, I exchanged looks with Di and Marie, wondering if, like me, they were now considering how we were supposed to go about that.

'I think it's odd that someone would make themselves a killer when all they have to do is wait,' offered Di with an apologetic smile.

I nodded faintly to agree and wondered if anyone else was feeling uncomfortable dealing with the subject of Geraldine's demise.

'Well maybe it's because I've hinted that I'm going to change my will. In France you can't disinherit your children but I'm planning to make a will using English law which the French authorities will respect when I'm gone as I'm a UK citizen. So I can leave this house and land to anyone I choose. My guess is therefore, that someone wants me dead before I've had a new will prepared.'

I suddenly got the feeling that Geraldine's drip feeding of information was deliberate, as if she was purposely holding back details she didn't need to tell us unless it was absolutely necessary. This latest morsel was given in the hope that it would convince us of her theory but I still had my doubts. Someone in the family had supposedly poisoned the cat and now wanted to kill its owner seemed to be founded on a note left with the cat which Geraldine hadn't shown to anyone and claimed she'd since lost then a second note which had a childlike drawing of hangman. I regarded her thoughtfully while she discussed with the others her need to rest between her medical treatments. What else was she keeping from us? Was there anything she was determined not to share?

'My plan,' Geraldine was saying, 'is to say that Marie's visit with her friends, that is, you two, was prearranged and you are here to have a break from your usual routine and to get away from it all. Keep an element of truth so that if anyone questions you, you can reply honestly. Then if anyone checks up on you Catherine, they'll see reports of the murders in your hamlet or more specifically in your *chambres d'hotes* which will confirm your need to recharge your batteries, as it were.'

I nodded slowly, wondering how to even begin to approach the task she'd set.

'I think you might need to gain their trust.' Geraldine continued. 'But also, being from outside the family, I think they might open up to you since they'll not see you as a threat to their precious inheritance.'

She looked at Di. 'And of course, if you pool your information we can really find out who it is that's threatening my life.'

'And what will you do if we find out who wrote the notes and poisoned the cat? After all, in the eyes of the law no crime has really been committed. Even the notes can't be actually seen as threats.'

Geraldine pondered for a moment. 'I shall confront them, explain how hurtful it was for them to kill my cat and of course make sure they are written completely out of my will.'

Just then there was a knock on the door. Collette poked her head around it. 'The doctor's here.' She said in perfect, unaccented English. 'Thank you Collette I'll be right there.' She turned to us, a weary look on her face. 'I must go. Please take your time to finish up here and Collette will be around to show you to your room. Just a little tinkle of the bell and she'll come running.'

As Geraldine left the room, Marie smiled apologetically at our bemused expressions.

'*Je suis vraiment désolée*. I honestly didn't know about all this. Geraldine told me she wanted some support while she had some of her children visit. I knew about the English ones and how they had come to resent her, and I knew that there was a problem between Geraldine and her daughter Irène, but I didn't know where it stemmed from.' She thought for a moment, her eyes widening. 'I certainly did not know that Julien had a different father or that Henri's other children's sole reason for being here was because they were expecting something from a will. Nor did I know that there actually *wasn't* a will.'

'There seems to be a lot of inconsistencies' I began thoughtfully. Di interrupted. 'You already told us that Geraldine was a friend of your mother's. How did they become friends exactly?'

'When Geraldine first moved to the area she needed some translation work doing, usual stuff you need when trying to settle into a new country. My mother helped her out and they became good friends.'

'But, alas not good enough that Geraldine would trust her with a secret about her sham marriage.' Observed Di.

Marie shook her head in dismay but said earnestly. '*C'est étrange, mais* my mother told me once that if I ever needed any help, no matter what, I could always count on Geraldine so I trust her implicitly. If she says her life is in danger, then I believe her.'

Still feeling cynical, I changed the subject. 'So you must have lived in this area when you were young Marie? I mean if Geraldine has lived here the whole time and your mother helped her?'

Marie nodded. 'We left here when I was very young. My father was not the best husband to my mother, I don't know exactly what he did, but she let things slip from time to time. One day we just upped and left the area and never returned.'

I suddenly felt sorry for Marie. 'I didn't realise.'

Marie shook her head. 'No reason you should. And it has not affected me. I lived a happy life with my mother and siblings.'

'Have you never wanted to get in touch with your father? As an adult I mean? Maybe he still lives in the area.' Said Di.

'*Non*, I had no interest in meeting up with him and my mother told me that he had died sometime after we left anyway.'

'And what about anyone who knew him after you left, or any other family he had. Aren't you just a little bit curious about what became of him?' Persisted Di.

Marie shrugged. 'I know his name but have no desire to seek out any other information about him.'

Marie's comment brought the conversation to an end, so we followed Geraldine's advice and summoned Collette who promptly showed us to our shared room.

The room itself was charming. It was painted in warm beige tones and spacious enough to fit in a four-poster bed on one side and two single beds on another without feeling cramped. A large teak armoire dominated the wall adjacent to the bathroom, which we were amazed to discover was almost totally comprised of white marble giving it a luxurious and elegant feel. After taking some time to marvel and express delight at our lavish surroundings, we prepared to settle in for our stay. While we moved clothing from our bags into our allotted drawers and arranged toiletries I wondered about the circumstances surrounding Henri's death and queried it with Marie. Assuming my interest was because I thought it might have been suspicious, she assured me that it was all above board. Henri had by all accounts had a weak heart and had gone peacefully in his sleep. I nodded, digesting the information and deciding that at least Geraldine's concerns about her own welfare weren't a result of her husband's cause of death.

CHAPTER TWO

Waking early and well before the others the next morning I lay surveying the shadows cast by the furnishings in the muted light of the room. I mulled over the discussion about Geraldine's fears we'd had during the previous afternoon, while enjoying a walk through the grounds and the adjacent park. Inadvertently my thoughts jumped to the cold chicken salad Collette had been good enough to prepare for our dinner, the images of which causing my stomach to rumble. Without another thought I rose, got dressed and headed down to the kitchen in search of breakfast.

*

I found Collette rinsing dishes in the kitchen. She glanced up in surprise as I entered before her round, kindly face creased into a broad smile.
'*C'est tot* Madame!'
'*Oui, mais j'ai très faim.*'
We exchanged grins at our shared joke: communicating in French when we both knew she could converse just as fluently in English. Collette gestured toward a large open carton of eggs on the counter between us.
'Fresh from my chickens this morning. Would you like some?'
I beamed a smile. 'That would be lovely thank you.'

I watched as she began to prepare coffee, refusing my offer of help before ushering me into the dining room and then shortly after, serving me with slices of crusty loaf and poached eggs. She left the room only to return minutes later to place a basket of warm croissants next to a pot of hot coffee.

I was focused on mopping up yolk with a piece of bread when a man entered the room. He started on seeing me, clearly not expecting to see anyone else around so early. My mouth full, I simply lifted a hand in greeting.

His eyes took in the food laid out on the table before casting a swift glance in my direction. Then, with a barely perceptible nod he turned on his heel and left the room. And good morning to you too I thought. My appetite satisfied; I took my coffee to a more comfortable seat on the sofa at the far end of the dining room.

Despite the Wi-Fi being patchy, I managed to spend time checking emails on my phone. As eight o'clock approached, I heard more movement in the house with Marie being the next visitor to the dining room. She smiled in surprise and glanced at the dishes on the table.

'*Eh bien*, you've eaten already? Must've been up early.'

I nodded. 'With the larks. Luckily Collette was around, and I'm pleased to say served me with a delicious breakfast.'

Marie looked pleased. 'She's busy now preparing more food but wouldn't let me help, I think she sees the kitchen as her domain and won't allow anyone else to take over.'

Marie took a seat at the table. I moved to sit next to her and kept my voice low. 'Someone else came in earlier, a man, didn't seem too happy to see anyone else in here and left without saying a word.'

'What did he look like?'

'Medium height, dark wavy hair, slim, in his forties I think.'

'Sounds like Julien. Collette just told me he and Genevieve as well as David arrived late last night. David is tall and not as dark.'

We both turned on hearing someone else enter the room. Di smiled a good morning and sat down next to us.

'Sleep well?' Asked Marie.

'Like a log,' breathed Di.

Collette entered the dining room just then with fresh coffee and pastries.

'*Merci bien* Collette,' said Marie.

Collette returned her smile before going back to the kitchen.

*

After breakfast we returned to our room and set about preparing a plan of attack. We agreed that if we were to make any headway in discovering who was threatening Geraldine, then time was of the essence. Di pointed out that as our plan had been to stay for a maximum of seven days, we would need a strategy which started immediately. I proposed the only way to accomplish anything would be to inveigle our way into the family's confidence. The three of us were outwardly enthusiastic about our chances of success but the doubts I had of achieving anything in such a short space of time I kept to myself.

'We might need to start by finding out about the circumstances surrounding the poisoned cat,' proposed Di.

'Hm, yes, we need to confirm that all family members were staying here at the time of the funeral and if anyone can shed any light on the note found with it.'

'Did Geraldine say she'd shown anyone else the second note, I'm thinking of this Inspector Borné in particular?' Asked Di.

I frowned trying to recall what exactly Geraldine had said.

'I don't remember,' mumbled Marie almost to herself.

'Did she say she didn't bother showing him because he wasn't interested in the first one or did she say she'd lost it so never got a chance?'

Di and Marie murmured indistinctly and we all frowned trying to recall her exact words.

'Unless, she meant she lost the first one,' I mumbled, recalling the facts about the note were a bit unclear.

'Why don't we allocate a specific family member to work on, you know, try to gain their confidence.' Suggested Marie, dismissing the note as unimportant.

'If only a few of the family have turned up so far, I'm wondering how we'll be able to do it in the little time we have.' Said Di.

I nodded. 'And if the rest of them don't turn up until later in the week, we'll not have much time to question them without it being obvious that we're doing so.'

'I'll have a word with Geraldine today to see if she can tell me exactly when everyone is arriving.' Said Marie.

'Maybe Lesley and Sophie can play a part somehow.' I wondered aloud. 'After all, they're heading down here tomorrow for a couple of nights, maybe there might be something they could do too.'

'*Oui, mais*, I'm not sure how they could be of use but it's something to consider.' Nodded Marie.

'How about we just introduce ourselves today to any family already here, you know, get a feel for the situation?' Suggested Di.

I smiled. 'Good idea, we could head back downstairs and see if we can find anyone that we can chat to without any particular agenda.'

As we readied ourselves to leave the room I said.

'Incidentally Marie, doesn't *borné* mean...?'

She grinned and nodded. '*Exactement.*'

Di looked at me for clarification.

'Inspector *Borné*. Thick headed.'

Di registered the meaning with raised eyebrows and a slow smile of amusement.

'By the sounds of it,' I mused. 'If what Geraldine says is true then he's aptly named.'

'Hm, it does make you wonder what else he hasn't bothered to investigate.'

*

As we reached the hallway we spied Collette in discussion with a tall, slim man with dark wavy hair and whose back was toward us. Wondering if their conversation might have some relevance I halted on our way to the dining room to fake interest in a family photograph hanging on the wall. Marie and Di, momentarily surprised, quickly guessed my intentions and huddled around it with me as we made a show of examining the subjects in the frame. The subterfuge allowed us to overhear details about Geraldine's medication and a reminder from the man, who I now surmised to be the doctor, that Geraldine's confused state would only worsen. It occurred to me as he spoke that the open and rhythmic intonation of his accent meant he was likely to be 'Marseillais'. I knew this because Marie had once coached me in various markers of French accents and explained how spoken French from Marseille was distinct from other French speakers, explaining that they tended to add 'eh' to the end of their sentences. Stealing a quick glance toward Collette and the visitor again, I saw her nodding to his instructions and overheard her assure him that the medication would be given according to his directions. She also assured him that she would encourage Geraldine to get plenty of rest without interruptions or stress from her guests.

We continued to loiter as Collette and the doctor, ignoring us, walked past us to the front door, still deep in conversation. We turned to stare, as she closed the door behind him then headed back toward the kitchen, smiling briefly in our direction as she passed. We waited for a minute or two before deeming it safe to comment.

'So, Collette is responsible for giving Geraldine her medication.' Stated Di in a harsh whisper.

Marie and I gazed at her and nodded though I suspected none of us had found the information to have any particular relevance.

'How shall we...?' Started Marie after a few moments of silence.

'Split up maybe?' I suggested.

Di was nodding in agreement. 'See who's around.'

We each went our separate ways, wandering through the downstairs rooms in search of family members, only to be disappointed to find the rooms empty. While Di and I lingered in the dining room, Marie resorted to approaching Collette in the kitchen, feigning innocent interest in the meal she was busy preparing. Collette, without prompting, informed Marie that Geraldine had asked her to prepare for dinner for ten for that evening. She also indicated that Geraldine was expecting Marie and her guests to attend. As this had to mean more family members would be arriving that same day, we decided our quest for information might yet prove fruitful.

CHAPTER THREE

There were brief introductions as we took our seats for dinner with the rest of the family. Ann, Billy and Celia appeared openly friendly, David and Elise, though not unfriendly gazed at me and Di curiously while Genevieve studied the three of us, offering only a tight smile just as Collette entered the room alongside a woman who bore a striking resemblance to Geraldine. The woman, I took to be Irène greeted

Marie warmly, kissing on both cheeks before greeting me and Di in the same way.

As Collette placed baskets of bread on the table a younger woman arrived with extra cutlery and busied herself arranging it on each place setting. Then Collette and her assistant, who I took to be Malarie, came back and forth into the room carrying plates laid out with the *entrée* consisting of slices of pork and mushroom *terrine* served with *cornichons* and baby salad leaves.

Small talk began with Irène asking Celia how long she, Billy and Anne had taken to drive down from the St Malo ferry then expressing polite surprise that David and Elise had turned up earlier than expected. In the meantime Billy took it upon himself to move around the table filling wine glasses.

I took a sip just as I caught a glimpse of a black cat wandering through the room.

Di brought attention to it. 'Oh I see Geraldine has another cat.'

The comment was not lost on the family who gazed at Di with a mixture of surprise and suspicion, the ensuing silence making me feel distinctly uncomfortable.

'Just the one cat, as always,' said Celia with an amicable smile.

Marie reached for a piece of bread and frowning, said to no one in particular, '*Tout à fait*, but we were told the cat died.'

The family traded wary looks but said nothing.

'I think you've been misled.' Interjected Julien who came swaggering into the room at that precise moment. He helped himself to wine before taking a seat opposite his fiancée, Genevieve. Strangely, the look she gave him was anything but friendly.

Taking a large mouthful of wine, he returned Genevieve's look with one of defiance before turning to gaze directly at Di.

'Di, is it?'

She nodded.

'You do know the meds our dear mother is on can cause paranoia.'
'So you think Geraldine is confused about this?' Asked Marie innocently.
Julien smirked and circled his finger toward his temple in a gesture generally meant to suggest insanity.
Irène coughed, 'I don't think that's entirely fair Julien, she is after all very ill, so she needs the medication whether it has side effects or not.' Anne and Celia nodded in agreement. Before anyone else had a chance to say anything, Geraldine shuffled into the room. She looked pale and tired, so different from when we'd spoken the day before and was leaning heavily on a cane. Everyone apart from Julien and Genevieve moved immediately, intent on offering assistance. Geraldine waved a hand of dismissal.
'I came to offer my apologies' she said gazing around the table, 'I don't feel as well as expected so will forego having dinner with you all.' She glanced at us three before adding. 'Please look after our guests won't you. I'm hoping to see you in the morning for breakfast but for now I need to rest.'
The mood was subdued after Geraldine's brief visit, bringing it to everyone's attention how ill she actually was. However, after several minutes, everyone's attention gradually returned to the impending meal and the small talk began again. While everyone was attempting pleasantries I noted several disapproving glances thrown toward Julien who was busy scrolling through his mobile phone.
When a discussion began about Celia's children and how they were settling into new classes at school and expressions of surprise made about their increasing age, Genevieve sighed audibly, making Irène roll her eyes.
'Why is it that you came Julien?' Asked Elise as if emboldened by Irène's look of disapproval.

Julien glanced up from his phone, his eyes narrowing on her face.
'Came to see what the old man left me, if anything, the same reason as everyone else I expect.'
Elise stared at him with a look of distaste.
'But none of us brought our other halfs except you Julien, why is that?' Elise's tone was mocking and she deliberately avoided Genevieve's indignant look.
Julien sneered. 'What you mean is you're upset because Bruno,' he paused to gaze slowly around the group for dramatic effect, 'husband *number four,* didn't want to come with you? Maybe you should start looking for candidate number five.'
Elise' face reddened suddenly and she exploded with a string of expletives. David meanwhile, in a show of support for his sister, rose quickly from his chair and lunged at Julien while hurling accusations of slander. Glassware toppled over onto dishes as Billy jumped up to separate them with Anne and Celia issuing pleas for calm.
Unexpectedly, the two sides quickly saw sense and did as instructed, with peace being restored just as quickly as hostilities had erupted. When Collette arrived moments later, followed closely by Malarie pushing a hostess trolley, the family appeared outwardly composed despite the odd resentful glance across the table. Once the hot dishes were placed in the centre of the table, we were left to our meal.
The brooding calm made me feel distinctly uncomfortable and Di, Marie and I traded awkward glances whereupon Irène took it upon herself to apologize that we had been forced to witness a demonstration of their dysfunctional family. Luckily no one showed any reaction to her apology with everyone focused on eating in silence. We helped ourselves in turn to the beef *cassoulet* and vegetables and after several minutes Anne and Celia attempted once again to make polite conversation. Julien snorted in disgust on hearing one remark but after a dark look from Billy, made no further comment and simply

sat with a scowl making it obvious he was sulking. David and Elise kept their tones civil and neither looked in Julien's direction for the rest of dinner. Genevieve meanwhile refused to speak to anyone.
As soon as Genevieve finished her main course, she took her leave with Julien muttering under his breath as he followed her out. That he was trying to have the last word by accusing Elise of causing Genevieve's distress was not lost on the group who seemed to visibly relax after his departure. A short while later we were pleased to be enjoying pear tart for dessert with freshly roasted coffee in a much more genial atmosphere.

*

'Well we certainly got a good feel for the family dynamic this evening,' declared Di once we reached our room.
'Yes we were left with little doubt about where the allegiances lie.' Nodded Marie.
'I wonder if David and Julien have a certain amount of respect for Billy or maybe they just respect him for his size.'
'Yeah I wouldn't want to tackle him,' agreed Di.
'It does look as though he's seen a few fights in his time,' I looked at Marie who as expected, filled us in on his background. 'He was a boxer when he was young and not bad at it by all accounts.'
I nodded. 'Ah, I thought, the shape of his nose gave that away.'
Di frowned. 'There wasn't much love lost between Elise and Julien though was there? I mean where did all that blow up from?'
'Hm some animosity there definitely.' I agreed.
'Looks like we're no further forward with any info on the poisoned cat though, if it is in fact true,' said Di.
'Yeah, starting to wonder if Julien, despite his unpleasant character, is right about Geraldine imagining it.' I added.

We both looked at Marie expecting some comment, but she was simply staring absently ahead as if lost in thought.

CHAPTER FOUR

We descended for breakfast the next morning to find the house deserted apart from Collette. She informed us that Geraldine was expecting us to join her for breakfast in the conservatory.
The conservatory was a room I found to be an absolute delight. Its walls were made of metal framed glass panes, one of which was half hidden by a long rustic potting bench filled with terracotta pots of varying sizes and foliage. Plants were crammed into every spare corner, hanging from above or standing tall, with others framing a large round distressed wooden table in the centre of the room. Fortunately Geraldine was looking more her usual self and sitting at part of the table in which some large green fern fronds were trying to lay claim. As we pulled out our heavy padded chairs to take our seats, I gazed upward to admire a large chunky chandelier made up of several pendant style candle holders. Geraldine was watching my face. I smiled at her. 'This is a beautiful room; I really am envious.'
She beamed. 'I thought you would like it in here, Marie told me you're a keen gardener.'
The table was laden with pastries, breads, and jams but no sooner had we sat down than Collette entered the room bringing a metal hot plate holding freshly scrambled eggs.

'Newly laid eggs,' Geraldine announced.
Marie smiled amicably. '*Merveilleux!* They were delicious yesterday.' Collette beamed, 'I have to bring them here as my family can't cope with them all.' She placed the hotplate down carefully and recommended caution before disappearing to fetch tea and coffee.
'She really is a dear,' said Geraldine fondly.
'Her English is impeccable. How long has she worked for you?' I asked.
Geraldine nodded. 'In response to both, she has an English father and has worked here about five years. Henri and I could manage this house ourselves up until then, apart from extra help in the garden of course. We decided to pay someone to help out with a little bit of cleaning and cooking, especially when we have guests.'
'So, you have a gardener?' Asked Di.
'Oh yes, Aldert, a lovely Dutch man, only been in France a few years. I couldn't have managed the garden without him. He's here four days a week and he works like a Trojan.'
As we chatted I noted there was a wealth of exotic plants in a far corner where the glass was showing signs of condensation due to its humid environment. Along one part glazed and part stone wall there stood a large wooden shelving unit and I was itching to get a closer look at the plants being propagated there since they seemed to be unsettlingly familiar.
'I see you've got your eye on my collection of toxic plants Catherine,' said Geraldine.
I stared at her. 'I wasn't sure, but it did seem as if they were all of a certain type. And,' attempting to finish my mouthful of scrambled egg I got up to take a closer look, 'I see you're also collecting the seeds.'
'I've also been studying them closely and have made extensive notes on each plant.' She grinned looking pleased with herself.

I glanced at a journal on the shelf, handwritten notes could be seen poking out between the pages.

'Is there a reason for the study?' Di asked without looking up while she spread jam onto a slice of *baguette*.

Geraldine shook her head. 'It's been an interest of mine for quite a while and since Henri died I've felt at a loose end, so decided to try to organize my notes into a book. Who knows, I may even get it published. You know there are a lot of French who die each year from mistaking poisonous plants from those which are edible. Some people even eat daffodil bulbs thinking they are onions would you believe?'

I shook my head nonplussed as I moved along to view the various plants.

'I'd heard that there are several deaths each year from people eating the wrong type of fungi after foraging too.' Said Di picking up her coffee cup.

I shuddered inwardly, reminded of an incident in which precisely that had happened.

'A book about them all sounds fascinating though,' Di was saying. 'Could you tell us about some of the plants you are cultivating here and their effects?'

I wondered if, like me, the poisoned cat had crossed Di's mind. Could someone inside the household have taken something toxic from Geraldine's collection?

'Is that a Brugmansia?' I interrupted before Geraldine had a chance to reply.

'Yes, also known as angel plant.' She explained for the benefit of the others.

'The flowers are quite beautiful,' said Di now getting up to take a closer look at the trumpet like flowers hanging from it.

'Careful Di, I think it's poisonous to touch.'

Geraldine nodded in agreement. 'Exposure to this Brugmansia species is highly poisonous and can cause anticholinergic syndrome in the central nervous system.'

Di looked shocked and returned immediately to her seat. She glanced at Marie who was busy dipping a *croissant* into her coffee. 'Think I'm better off over here.' She said, to which Marie smiled in response with a nod before taking a large bite.

I followed Di's lead and returned to my seat. 'Isn't every part of the angel trumpet highly poisonous? I mean leaves, flowers, seeds and roots?'

Geraldine nodded, pleased I assumed that she could converse with someone with some interest and knowledge of the plants she was cultivating.

'All of them contain the toxic alkaloids scopolamine, atropine and hyoscyamine, which are widely synthesized into modern medicinal compounds but of course are deadly poisonous if used outside a doctor's supervision.'

I nodded. 'I noticed you also have a packet of seeds over there for *Digitalis purpurea*.' I said as I poured myself a second cup of coffee.

'Dalmation Peach, yes, a foxglove.'

'Ah!' Piped up Marie who was now sitting back in her seat having eaten her fill. 'Ah *toxique*! I know that it is poisonous.' A smug grin sat on her face.

I nodded and allowed Geraldine to explain that foxgloves had a similar substance to digoxin so must not be eaten.

'I've read about digoxin poisoning' I added, 'I think it's a type of poisoning that can also occur in people who take too much of the medication digoxin as well as those who have eaten the plant.'

Geraldine nodded, smiling. 'That's very true but of course many plants which are regarded as unsafe for example, Belladonna, can be taken by mouth as a sedative, to stop bronchial spasms in asthma and whooping cough, and as a cold and hay fever remedy. It's also used for Parkinson's disease, colic, inflammatory bowel disease, motion sickness, and as a painkiller.'

I shook my head, amazed at her knowledge as well surprised at the plant's uses.

'Is that what they also call deadly nightshade?' Asked Marie with a worried frown. 'Someone told me I had some in my garden, but I was not sure what it looked like.'

'You can recognize it from the black glistening berries and vivid, reddish-purple leaves which are suspended from the stalk beneath the berries.' Explained Geraldine.

'I need to look out for that then.' Nodded Marie with a worried frown.

'I noticed when we took a walk through the garden that one of the espaliered apple trees, on the wall near the boathouse was draped in mistletoe.' I said.

'Ah yes' smiled Geraldine 'Mistletoe has great appeal in wintertime since it remains green and of course its berries ripen in December.'

'And isn't it also poisonous?' I asked.

Geraldine nodded. 'Yes, it can cause gastrointestinal upset from accidentally eating it'

'Maybe the cat could have eaten part of a plant and that's how it died?' Suggested Marie.

Geraldine looked alarmed and confused. 'No, I, er, no! It's one of *them*.' Warned Geraldine, lowering her voice while pointing toward the door. 'And you need to find out who it is!'

We glanced around at each other in surprise at her outburst, unsure how to respond. Finally Marie began to speak but Geraldine rose from her seat at the same time and cut her off. 'Now if you'll excuse me I need to rest.'

*

We decided questioning Jacques was a priority in order to find out the truth about the poisoned cat. As we'd already arranged to meet Lesley and Sophie in town, it was agreed that I would be the one to go and meet them while Marie and Di would seek out Jacques. Marie would then talk to Collette and Malarie afterwards to find out what they knew about Geraldine's family while Di could try to gain the confidence of some of the calmer members of the family, like Irène, Anne or Celia if they were around.

So, despite the threat of showers, it was just after midday when I set off at a leisurely pace along the narrow country road leading from Geraldine's house to walk into town.

CHAPTER FIVE

The plan was to meet Lesley and Sophie just before one for lunch on *rue Jean Jaurés* and having received a text message to say they were making good time and would be there soon, I announced my reservation at the small bistro before being shown to our table. Unfortunately, just as I sat down, I received another message from Lesley to say they'd been held up just outside Ruffec because of a *route barré*, meaning they'd been forced to join a queue of traffic making a long detour. Lesley assured me she would send regular updates as to their whereabouts. I sighed with disappointment just as the waiter arrived with the menu. Not wanting to lose our table since the bistro was quickly filling up, and reluctant to go out into what was now quite a downpour, I made a show of studying the dishes with great interest all the while wondering how long I could delay ordering any food.

Reading descriptions of the food did nothing to assuage my rumbling stomach and served only to make my mouth water. I stole a quick glance around the bistro and was met with curious stares. I presumed my taking up a table which could comfortably seat four was beginning to cause some resentment as the place was now full with a small queue forming at the entrance.

Another text message arrived just as the waiter reappeared which caused me some consternation; they'd had to follow a diversion which was proving to be well out of the way. Lesley said they were now about an hour behind time and suggested it might be prudent to meet for dinner instead. I quickly sent a thumbs up to agree and turned my attention to the waiter who was now hovering impatiently by my side.

'Madame?'

Making a split decision to sate my hunger, I told him there'd been a change of plan and I would be dining alone but would be needing a few more minutes to make my choice from the menu.

In the blink of an eye, the waiter had whisked away one half of the table and was now setting the new table up about a metre away with cloth and tableware, while another waiter appeared from nowhere to take two of the chairs. Seconds later a family of four was being ushered from the entrance toward the table and despite the squeeze around it, chattered happily, seeming thankful to be seated.

I ordered a sparkling mineral water and decided to opt for the *menu du jour*, which started with a mushroom paté and was followed by poached salmon.

While waiting for my food I took out a notepad with the intention of ordering my thoughts and jotting down anything I deemed was relevant information.

Raised voices and raucous laughter caused me to throw a cursory glance across the room. Observing a family group in high spirits made me smile but not before I'd caught sight of a familiar face.

Julien was leaning against a bar stool while the bar tender poured him what looked like a glass of whiskey. They chatted as he was being served and from their body language and easy manner it was clear they knew each other. When Julien swivelled round to glance at the diners I quickly looked down at the notepad, elbow resting on the table and scratching an imaginary itch on my forehead to shield my face as I tried to avoid his attention.

Moments later I was forced to look up as a waiter arrived at my table with the starter. When he made no effort to move away, I gazed up at him quizzically. He seemed uneasy.

'Madame, as we are very busy, would it be too much of an imposition to ask you to share your table?'

I stared at him for a moment in surprise but then shrugged. Why not? 'No problem.'

He beamed. '*Merci* Madame.'

When I saw him gesture toward one of the bar staff, I squirmed. Surely I hadn't just agreed to let Julien share my table. Picking up cutlery and keeping my head down, I frantically sought for ways to renege on my offer, I really was not looking forward to another unpleasant meal alongside Julien.

'Madame Patterson?'

Recognising the voice, I glanced up in disbelief, instinctively beaming a huge smile.

A rather relaxed looking Inspector Maupetit, was staring down at me in equal surprise.

'Ah, I see you are acquainted.' The waiter said as he pulled out the chair opposite before scurrying off toward the bar. I felt myself visibly relax as it dawned on me that it was the Inspector who was about to share my table.

The Inspector however, remained standing while sweeping his eyes around the room.

Somewhat dumbfounded I stared at him, taking in his designer stubble and how his tanned skin contrasted sharply with the crisp whiteness of his shirt.

'You are here alone, *tout seule*?' He said finally, meeting my gaze.

I stuttered, 'yes, I, er, was supposed to be meeting friends but they've been caught up. Some traffic incident outside Ruffec apparently.'

He nodded in understanding. 'Ah, *oui*, a tractor I believe has shed its load across both lanes – a lot to clean up.'

He took hold of the back of the chair. 'You don't mind?'

Please take that seat I pleaded silently but simply smiled sweetly, 'of course not.'

He grinned, taking off his short brown suede jacket and placing it on the back of his chair before taking his seat. He then picked up the menu and handed it to a passing waiter.

'You're not eating?' I asked curiously.

'Already ordered. The chef is, *une vieille connaissance,* an old acquaintance so no need to go through the usual process.'

I stared at him, still taken aback by his presence. He responded by giving me a quizzical look. Reddening suddenly, I forced myself to look down at my food realizing I was clutching tightly onto my knife and fork, yet my food remained untouched.

'Please do not let me stop you.'

His friendly manner did nothing to alleviate my discomfort at the thought that I was about to eat while he watched. Fortunately, the waiter arrived with his food just as I started on mine. Without looking up I heard the Inspector thank the waiter by name and wondered how it was that he knew these people.

When the waiter reappeared moments later with a bottle of red wine, he poured a glass for the Inspector before pausing, clearly waiting for me to accept some. My mouth full, I frowned and shook my head. The

Inspector, thanked the waiter and asked him to leave the bottle on the table. With a faint look of surprise, the waiter did as instructed.

'You are driving?' Asked the Inspector.

'No, no, just wanted to keep a clear head.'

'Ah,' he nodded then took a sip of wine and I suddenly realized this was the first time I'd ever seen him taking some time off from his work.

When a different waiter stopped at our table to ask if the wine was acceptable, I glanced up to see the Inspector wink and smile in response. After several minutes of silence while we ate, I glanced up curiously to discover the Inspector tucking into his food with relish and noticed that he was enjoying a dish that I couldn't recall seeing listed on the menu.

'*C'est comment?* Your food?' He asked after catching my look.

'Good, yes, very good.' I nodded.

His focus was then taken up with mopping up some of the sauce on his plate with bread. 'Hugo *est un excellent cuisinier*, an excellent chef.'

I smiled, disarmed by his manner and relaxed a little, feeling that we were simply dining together as friends. There was no agenda, no need to talk about murders or suspects. We were simply enjoying a meal and happened to be at the same restaurant, at the same time and due to circumstances beyond our control, at the same table.

When finished, the Inspector sat back in his chair with a satisfied look while I took a sip of water. Sensing his gaze on me, I tried to hide my unease by taking my attention to the notepad, picking up the pen as if to begin writing.

'Your memoirs?'

I gazed up at him in surprise to find him smiling broadly.

'Mem..? No, no,' I laughed lightly.

The waiter arrived then to take our dishes and the Inspector took the opportunity to lean forward, inclining his head to better see what was written.

Not wanting him, or anyone else for that matter to read my stream of consciousness, I quickly flipped the cover to hide my notes.

Unperturbed, he simply shrugged, sighed contentedly, took a sip of wine and leaned back in his seat once again, gazing absently around the room.

I changed the subject. 'So, you know the waiter too?'

He nodded, smiling faintly. '*Un veil ami.*'

'Oh, so you're here to visit old friends?'

The Inspector narrowed his eyes, but he remained relaxed, a slow grin spreading across his face.

'Am I being interrogated Madame Patterson?'

Reminded of a time when he'd mocked my suggestion that he interrogate a suspect and guessing he'd phrased the question in a way that showed he was also reminded of it, I simply shrugged and smiled, trying hard to refrain from taking his comment too seriously. 'Just making conversation.'

'Ah, *les banalités*, small talk,' he nodded. '*Et vous?* Is this simply a vacation with friends?'

I nodded, recognizing his response as a question – that was just like him; avoid giving any information yet trying to extract it from someone else. Well, two can play at that game, I thought and smiled enigmatically.

'Something like that.'

He made no comment but continued to study my face as if waiting for me to elaborate. However, I refused to be drawn and simply continued smiling cheerfully as I took my turn to gaze absently around the room. When our main course arrived, I enthused over it to avert any further questions. The Inspector, his expression unreadable yet still amicable, nodded faintly without further comment before starting on his food. I glanced up just as he went to pour himself another glass of wine. He threw me a questioning glance while holding onto the bottle to which I again shook my head.

It occurred to me that the conversation might have taken a different turn if I'd accepted the wine, but as it was, it was stilted. Our comments remained restricted to food, the surroundings and even more excruciating, the weather. When I received a text message to say that Lesley and Sophie were about to park the car and would meet me outside the *Saint André* church, within the following ten minutes, the Inspector seemed relieved to hear that I needed to leave and informed the waiter that he would take coffee at the bar. We then got up from the table simultaneously, he, to have coffee and me, so I could pay my bill at the till. When I heard the Inspector conversing quickly with someone in French as I was putting away my purse, I glanced across to see him with a huge grin on his face as he shook hands vigorously with the chef. Although not keen to intrude I stared at the chef who was facing me because I was sure I recognized him from an earlier encounter. Sensing my look he shifted his gaze, then with narrowed eyes he studied me for a moment.

'It's Cat'rine – I think?' He said, his face clearing.

'Ah yes!' I said, smiling with sudden recollection. This was Hugo, the chef from *Verteuil sur Charente* where Marie and I had had lunch on the way to the chateau family birthday party. Tales of Marie and his friendship flashed through my mind.

He glanced at the Inspector and seemed as if he was about to introduce us when the Inspector intervened.

'Madame Patterson and I have just dined together.'

'*Ah bon!* You know each other!' He threw a wink at the Inspector.

'You were lucky to have had a such a pretty dining guest Didier.'

Embarrassed by his comment I made a show of checking my watch. Then without glancing at the Inspector I thanked Hugo for preparing a delicious meal and told him I had to run, conscious of the Inspector's look of interest as I headed for the exit.

CHAPTER SIX

The rain had stopped and the sun had come out. A rainbow sat over the buildings opposite which lifted my mood as I stepped outside into clean, fresh air. I couldn't help but smile as I walked away from the main square, down the hill toward the church, my mind still filled with thoughts from the last few hours. As I neared our meeting place I spied Lesley and Sophie walking briskly toward me. We greeted each other warmly while they gushed with apologies over their lateness. I explained there was no need and that I'd still had an interesting lunch. Relieved, they explained that they still needed to check in at their hotel as they'd just left their overnight bags in the foyer with the receptionist before rushing to meet me and were concerned about leaving them there for too long. Agreeing it was better to return to their hotel so they could get the keys to their room we set off in that direction.

The hotel was situated just off the main square. While I waited for Sophie and Lesley to take the bags to their rooms, I surveyed the clean modern lines of the foyer appreciating the high standard of the decor. My hotel assessment was interrupted only minutes later when Sophie and Lesley returned expressing their delight at the condition and charm of their room. We then headed to the main square where they chose a pleasant little bistro in which to have dinner and made a reservation before we headed next door for coffee for a quick catch up.

'Tell us about your interesting lunch Catherine.' Urged Lesley just as our coffees were served.

I described my dining experience with Inspector Maupetit.
'But what a coincidence for him to be here!' Gasped Sophie.
I shrugged. 'He seemed to know the chef and a couple of the waiters.'
'Maybe he's from the area.' Offered Lesley.
'Could be,' I agreed just as I glimpsed Julien leaving the bistro next door. Sophie followed my gaze.
'What's up?'
I shook my head in confusion and lowered my voice. 'Not sure. One of Geraldine's sons, Julien has just gone into that bistro.' I paused.
'And?'
'And nothing really but he was also in the restaurant I had lunch in.'
'So he's particularly hungry today,' chuckled Lesley.
I smiled wryly. 'Actually I don't know whether he ate in there or not. I didn't notice.'
'Too busy sharing notes with the Inspector.' Said Lesley with a mischievous grin.
I threw an indignant look in her direction but decided her remark was meant innocently. Then, glimpsing Julien leave the bistro and march directly across the square to a restaurant opposite I shifted in my seat so I was almost hidden from his line of view. 'I certainly don't want him to come over to say hello because based on first impressions, I don't think he's a very pleasant character.'
'So that's three eateries he's visited.' Observed Sophie raising an eyebrow.
'Up to something d'you think?'
'Maybe,' she said, shrugging.
Lesley shook her head, bemused. 'Maybe you two are looking for mystery where there isn't any.'
I shared a surprised look with Sophie and we both grinned.
'Probably.' I said, making the decision not to comment on any more on Julien's comings and goings for the time being.

*

The sound of sirens grew louder as I reached the gate to Geraldine's house and my heart sank when a police car turned into the property. Faltering on my approach, I stared in horror as two more police cars sped to a halt outside the front door.
I watched as the scene unfolded with Malarie rushing out of the front door to brief them. Filled with dread, I came to a complete stop. How we had let Geraldine down! She'd put her faith in us, expecting us to tell her who was trying to kill her and we hadn't discovered anything! It struck me suddenly that there were no emergency medics. Why had only police turned up? Was it too much to wish it was a false alarm? Did I dare expect that an attempt on Geraldine's life had been unsuccessful?
Forcing myself to continue, I took a deep breath and continued toward the commotion. Malarie, after speaking urgently to the gendarmes, was now racing through the garden toward the back of the house with the officers in hot pursuit.
Billy, Marie and Elise appeared one after another at the front door to peer after them but strangely didn't seem to be offering any assistance. And by the time I reached the entrance, Billy and Elise had gone back inside as if from lack of interest. Meanwhile Marie, having seen my approach, offered me a weak smile.
I moved to embrace her in sympathy but she held back.
'What is it?'
'Geraldine?' I asked warily.
She shook her head vehemently. '*Non*, Geraldine's fine. It's Jacques.'
'What?' I struggled to understand.
'Malarie found him dead.'
Slowly registering her words I gazed at her in stunned silence.

'Let's talk about it inside,' Marie said quietly as she turned to go into the house.

'I thought…' I began, reluctant to voice my thoughts as I hurried to fall into step alongside.

'I know you did, but she's alright.'

Deciding we'd have more privacy to discuss events in our room we began to climb the stairs, noticing Di ahead of us. I was just about to call out to her when an uproar broke out below, forcing the three of us to turn toward the source at the foot of the stairs.

Malarie stood fuming and shouting accusations while waving her arms at an elderly man only steps away from her. She was threatening to sue him and proclaiming she would make it known to everyone how incompetent he was. Based on Geraldine's description of Inspector Borné and her claims of his earlier ineptitude, my guess was that this was the same detective. Regarding Malarie with pity, the Inspector was attempting to placate her but Malarie's stance became more and more aggressive, forcing two uniformed gendarmes to bridge the gap between her and their boss. Moments later Malarie made a lunge across them toward the Inspector but the officers acted quickly to restrain her. Meanwhile Anne and David, hovering close by, rushed over to intervene, persuading the officers that Malarie wasn't a threat and was acting only out of grief, explaining she was more in need of their pity than heavy handed tactics. Fortunately they saw their point of view and loosened their hold on Malarie who then fell into Anne's arms sobbing, before being gently led away.

The detective was left looking somewhat flustered but after a moment of reflection breathed a heavy sigh of relief, pulling awkwardly at the collar of his jacket. He then issued orders in hushed tones and the two officers left the room.

Casting an awkward glance around, the detective spotted us as shameless onlookers and hardened his expression to a glare.

Reluctantly we turned away and only managed to sneak a glance when we heard him head for the door. We did however, refrain from commenting until we were back in our room, talking simultaneously as we hurried to spill our thoughts.

'Hang on.' I urged as I opened my notebook and made myself comfortable on the bed. Di and Marie realizing at the same time that talking over each other wasn't helping, stopped speaking and waited patiently. With pen at the ready I looked from one to the other expectantly.

'So, maybe we should start with what just happened?' Proposed Di.

'Absolutely.' I said as Marie muttered in agreement.

'Ok I'll go first,' offered Marie, 'since I witnessed some of it.' She glanced at us both to check she had our agreement and full attention.

Di frowned. 'But maybe we should start with bringing Catherine up to date with events before that. They could be relevant and will keep the timeline right.'

I looked from one to the other in bemusement.

'But I can only guess at what all that drama was about!' I protested beginning to feel rather frustrated.

'Okay, okay, I'll explain this first then we'll cover the rest.' Said Marie.

Di sighed resignedly and nodded.

'Malarie found her father at the edge of the lake, face down in it, dead.'

'And I'm guessing the detective in charge said it was an accident. I mean that must be why she was making accusations about his competence because she thinks it wasn't an accident.'

'We're guessing so.' Marie and Di nodded.

'I overheard Malarie when she phoned the police saying it was obvious her father had a head wound. So I suppose it is plausible that he could have fell and hit it by accident.' Said Di.

'Hm. And I'm assuming that's the same Inspector? Borné? The one Geraldine was complaining about?'

Marie nodded.

'So Malarie *could* also be right about it being deliberate?'

Again they both nodded.

I looked down at the notebook and jotted down our theories with a question mark next to the information with the notion of visiting this later once a motive had been considered.

'So, do we have anything else to discuss? I mean did anyone manage to find out anything?'

They both started talking together again then Marie stopped, lifting her hand in a submissive gesture 'You go ahead.'

Di accepted graciously.

'Well, we decided to start with Jacques because we thought he would be the one to corroborate Geraldine's story about the cat. We found him at the lake, on his own.'

Marie nodded in agreement.

I sat patiently; pen poised.

'He was angry from the start. Said he knew who we were and had nothing to say to us. But we persisted and brought up the subject of the cat being poisoned. The problem was he denied any knowledge of it. Said he didn't know what we were talking about.'

'But we both thought he looked a bit shifty,' Agreed Marie, nodding.

'He did look genuinely baffled when we asked him about a note.' Added Di.

I looked between the two of them in bemusement. 'So are we saying it's looking likely that Geraldine made some, or all of it up?'

'Or is she confused?' Asked Marie with a sad look.

Di looked kindly at Marie. 'It must be the drugs she's on,' she offered.

'Did he say anything else? You know, maybe hearing about Geraldine's life being threatened?'

They both shook their heads. 'Didn't ask to be honest,' said Di.

'Mm…' I drew a line under my notes 'So that was it then…'

'Oh *non*,' interrupted Marie, 'there's more. I brought up the subject of the fishing license, asked him if Geraldine had agreed to issue another one. I was just making conversation really, trying to befriend him in the hope that he would open up to us.'

'Oh but surely that was a sore point? I mean if he knows she's not keen to continue with issuing the licenses.'

Marie was nodding. 'He said it was just spite that Geraldine was stopping him from fishing there and said Henri wouldn't have had a problem.'

'I suggested that Malarie might be able to persuade Geraldine since she was working for her but then that's when he turned nasty.' Added Di.

Marie nodded vehemently. 'Yes, he said he didn't want Malarie working for *that* family because they were trouble and that Malarie wouldn't need to ask because he could still get the fishing licence, no problem.'

I stared at them both. 'What did he mean by that?'

They both shrugged. 'He turned away from us and wouldn't say another word.' Said Di.

'I got the feeling he thought he'd said too much,' said Marie. Di nodded in agreement.

'So he was somehow confident he'd get the fishing license. I wonder what he was talking about when he said the 'family was trouble.''

We all fell silent for a few minutes while we considered what Jacques meant. With no suggestions forthcoming I broke the silence to change the subject. 'So tell me what happened next. How was Jacques found?'

'Actually something happened before that.' Said Marie.

I looked from Marie to Di.

'Yeah, I didn't hear this as I was out of earshot.' Said Di.

'Well,' continued Marie. 'I went to speak to Geraldine in her conservatory at the back of the house when we came back from the lake. I happened to walk in on an end of conversation with Julien, but it was clear he was in a foul mood.'

'Having been told about Henri not being his father maybe?'

Marie shrugged and continued. '*En tout cas*, Genevieve had been looking for Julien and got to the conservatory just as I did. All I heard was her saying 'Ah Elise told me you were here'. Then he ignored both her and me and left as if in a sulk. He went out through the outside conservatory door, with Genevieve hurrying to keep up with him.'

'Toward the garden?' I asked.

'Toward the lake.' Added Di conspiratorially.

'So Julien must've returned from the restaurant fairly quickly.'

They both looked at me curiously.

'I saw him when I was waiting for Sophie and Lesley – ended up having lunch with Inspector Maupetit of all people.'

I quickly put up my hand to stem their questions 'Long story which I can tell you about later but for now, what happened next?'

Di responded. 'Well that's it. Not long after we heard Malarie shouting and screaming for someone to call a doctor and coincidentally, it was only minutes later that Geraldine's doctor arrived at the house.'

'Mm, unfortunately Jacques was already dead and I think that's where you came in. So you know as much as we do now,' added Marie.

I nodded slowly digesting the information so far.

'What about Malarie?' I asked. 'Do we know if she was on friendly terms with her father?'

'Oh you mean as a suspect?' Stared Marie incredulously.

'Suppose it's possible,' said Di looking at us both doubtfully as if this was the first time she'd considered the possibility. 'But in the short time we've been here I've not heard of any animosity between the two of them.'

'Of course we shouldn't get ahead of ourselves.' I cautioned. 'We don't know whether Jacques' death was deliberate or not. Maybe we should wait and see before jumping to conclusions.'

Di nodded in agreement. 'And then consider what the motive might be.'

I added some notes to my book before looking up at Marie.

'Okay then, what, if anything, did you find out from Geraldine?'

'Well I tried to find out more details about the cat and the note but to be honest I didn't get the chance. She was keener to ramble on about some other guy called Veejay? Or maybe V.J.? She was incoherent, saying she shouldn't have trusted him. Then on hearing the commotion that went with Malarie finding her father, I didn't get a chance to question her further as Geraldine became very distressed about what happened to Jacques.'

'I wonder if she thought that it was meant to be her?' Suggested Di hesitantly.

I shrugged, wondering if how we were going to be able to see through the fiction and work out what were the facts. 'We'll have to continue investigating when things calm down, but I do hope we're not on some wild goose chase about this cat.'

CHAPTER SEVEN

Di phoned Sophie and Lesley at their hotel to let them know we were expected to stay at Geraldine's house for dinner. Despite voicing their disappointment that we weren't going to meet up, they accepted that being around the family was the priority.

While the three of us changed for dinner we discussed my lunch with the Inspector, agreeing that it would be interesting to find out why he was in Ruffec.

I told them about how familiar he'd been with the serving staff and that I'd been surprised to find out that he was friends with Hugo. Marie said that she knew Hugo had, a few months earlier, taken over as chef in a restaurant in the area but hadn't known which one. She explained that he and the Inspector went way back but didn't know how the Inspector would know the waiters at the restaurant. Lesley suggested that maybe Inspector Maupetit was from the area but Marie refuted the idea.

Turning our attention to Julien, we agreed that his behaviour seemed odd and none of us could come up with any idea as to why he was flitting from one restaurant to another without staying long enough to dine.

As to the suggestion that Julien had gone out into the garden toward the lake just before Jacques had been found, we agreed Julien seemed to be a likely suspect but we had no idea what his motive could be.

*

The mood in the dining room was sullen. Malarie was understandably absent with everyone pitching in to help Collette serve dinner. Julien and Genevieve, however, balked at the idea, thinking it beneath them. In fact, I thought Julien seemed rather distracted as well as subdued, I assumed because he was still reeling from Geraldine's revelation. Geraldine was not expected to join us but entered the dining room just as we began eating. Everyone listened attentively when she announced that Inspector Borné would be arriving the following morning to begin his enquiries into Jacques' death. Anne, Irène and David looked appalled at the thought and began to protest but Geraldine was adamant.

'I've requested he makes a proper investigation. Malarie cannot simply accept her father died and not know the reason why.'

'So we are to be questioned *even* though it was an accident?' Asked Elise indignantly.

'The police must not just assume there was no foul play!' Stated Geraldine forcefully. 'The *incident* needs to be thoroughly investigated.'

'Surely the Inspector should've questioned everyone today, when the scene was still fresh so to speak.' Remarked Billy.

'Yes well, he didn't seem too interested, yet again, so I made a formal request to his superior, which has been granted.'

'What do you mean *again*?' Asked Irène curiously.

'The cat being…'

'Not this again!' Exploded Julien.

'Enough Julien!' Demanded Celia.

'This family is truly insane!' Said Julien as he got up from the table and stormed out of the room. Genevieve rose quickly to follow him. Both meals were left half eaten, their cutlery left askew on the plates. Everyone else continued with their meal as if inured to the drama and Geraldine simply sighed and took a seat. Silence ensued and I wondered if we would ever get through an evening meal during our stay which we could class as pleasant. Irène was the first to try small talk, for which most of us were grateful but Geraldine, after serving herself with a few potatoes and pushing them round her plate, announced she needed to rest. Several of the family got up to offer her support but she shooed them away and left the room independently albeit leaning heavily on her walking stick.

There were some vain attempts at light conversation during the rest of dinner but the mood remained sullen. I also noticed the wine was going down at a steady rate as everyone seemed to be using it to drown out the horrors of the day.

'We were supposed to be here for the reading of the will.' Said Julian sulkily, returning to the room once Geraldine had gone.

'Well Mum isn't exactly well enough for that to happen so maybe it'll have to be postponed.' Anne replied, glancing anxiously around at others for support.

Julien snorted in disgust as he went to pour himself a drink from a whiskey bottle on the sideboard. 'Anyway, is this something we need to discuss with outsiders?'

'Julien!' Reprimanded Elise looking aghast.

Julien downed his whiskey and refilled it before gesturing in my direction. 'I've heard about Catherine Patterson and her *chambres d'hotes* of doom.'

'*Comment?*' Gasped Marie, shocked.

'And you needn't talk' He jabbed a finger toward Marie. 'You seem to encourage her. Yes, I've read all about you lot!' He waved a hand dismissively at the three of us.

Irène turned to us. 'I apologise for our brother.'

'Uh, no need to apologise when it's the truth,' declared Julien as he tried to wave his hand while holding the glass, causing his drink to slosh out of the glass. He leaned against the sideboard. 'And I for one won't associate with people whose entertainment is surrounding themselves with murderers,' he said spitefully, pushing himself upright and picking up the whiskey bottle before walking unsteadily from the room.

Di and I exchanged awkward looks while the rest of the family also glanced uneasily at each other.

Celia looking anxious, gave me a weak smile. 'Sorry you had to be spoken to like that. It was unforgiveable.'

'He's out of control,' said Billy shaking his head in disgust.

David sat silent, a dark look on his face.

Marie assured everyone that an apology wasn't necessary although once we finished our meal, sensing none of us would be keen to linger with the family, she made our excuses and we beat a hasty retreat back to our room.

CHAPTER EIGHT

Irène came to inform us while we were having breakfast that Inspector Borné had arrived and requested we all stay in the dining room until we were called. At that moment, she said he was speaking with Geraldine.

Collette came in then with a fresh pot of coffee and placed it on a sideboard.

'So you're staying for a few more days?' I heard Elise ask Di as they got up from the table together to get coffee.

Di smiled brightly. 'Yes. And you?'

Elise shrugged good naturedly but glanced around to see who was within earshot before she spoke. 'Well I'm not sure really. I thought we were all sort of summoned here to hear the contents of my father's will but you know,' she lowered her voice 'I don't even think he had one.'

'Here under false pretences I think,' muttered Anne quietly and casting a sideways look toward Billy.

Di waited for Elise to finish filling her cup and was about to respond but was cut off when David interrupted.

'We know he had nothing.' He said, picking up the coffee pot and looking pointedly at Di.

'Oh?' She asked innocently.

Elise looked surprised by the interruption but that changed to irritation when David seemed cavalier about disclosing subsequent family confidences.

'I'm quite sure Geraldine doesn't know that *we* know he had nothing.' David was saying, making no attempt to lower his voice and ignoring the scowl on Elise's face. 'You see our dear mother had a gambling problem and he bailed her out of several large debts over the years. We found this out later of course as our mother turned to us for money once we were of working age.'

The room was now silent with no one even pretending not to eavesdrop. Conscious of this audience, David gazed around defiantly. 'So now you all know our circumstances.'

He turned back to address his sister. 'And I for one have accepted that our father left us nothing, so the only thing we'd be entitled to is our share of this house.'

Under normal circumstances with the death of one parent, a share of the house would be automatically theirs as I knew that according to French law, half the family home is shared between the children with the surviving spouse keeping the other half. But since Geraldine and Henri weren't married I couldn't help but wonder how they stood to gain from the property. David's comment also made me wonder how keen they would be to get rid of Geraldine. Maybe they were impatient for her to meet her maker.

'Not wanting to sound materialistic,' muttered Genevieve, 'but I wonder how much this house is actually worth.'

Several family members ignored her comment, I guessed due to finding the subject rather distasteful. Irène however, gazed openly at Genevieve. 'If Geraldine has an English will, which can take precedence, she could disinherit all of us.'

This morsel of information instantly caused some consternation. Celia, Billy and Anne traded surprised glances, David and Elise gazed at

other with more shock than surprise and Genevieve smirked. Julien's responded by giving Irène a contemptuous look.
'Did I mention I saw Pascal a few weeks ago?'
Irène's face darkened, leading me to assume that Pascal was the man in her past, the one Geraldine had scared off.
When Irène didn't respond Julien continued regardless. '*Oui*, he was in a café with his wife, I didn't say hello as they were so busy making eyes at each other I didn't want to interrupt.'
Despite Irène's stony expression she didn't dignify Julien's comment with a response, choosing instead to leave the room.
Elise glared at Julien 'Must you be so insensitive?' She hissed.
Julien smirked and shrugged. 'Just making conversation.'
There were a few exasperated sighs at his conduct, and I saw Celia shake her head. However, from the lack of voiced criticism I guessed everyone was keen to let the matter drop.

The interviews were being conducted in the living room and as there was no particular person requested by the Inspector, it seemed to be whoever stood up the quickest when the next person was summoned. Agreeing it was better to allow family members to go first, we hung back hoping to catch any comments made on the way in or out of the interviews.
We overheard several interviewees report that the Inspector had refused to make use of one of the family as an interpreter. This resulted in Geraldine's oldest children, the English speaking family members who were no longer confident conversing in French, communicating with him by ridiculous methods such as charades.
We were, however, rewarded for our patience by overhearing Celia tell Anne that she'd disclosed to the Inspector that she'd seen the doctor in the grounds having a heated conversation with Jacques.

Stressing that she spoke in a sort of franglais because she couldn't remember a lot of the French words and just had to hope the Inspector understood her. Anne shook her head in bemusement and explained that Irène had mentioned that the doctor sometimes walked through the grounds as a short cut on his way home.

Since the Inspector asked for the doctor to answer some questions straight after the family members were finished, we assumed he'd understood what Celia had said. Once the family members had all been interviewed, only Me, Marie and Di were left waiting while the doctor was in the room so we moved closer to listen at the door.

The doctor was heard telling Inspector Borné that he'd chatted to Jacques about the weather.

'Did you talk about anything else?'

'*Non*, nothing else.' Replied the doctor.

The interview concluded swiftly and on hearing footsteps nearing the door, we dashed away from it, quickly trying to feign interest in various items decorating the hallway.

We were then called in one by one with the Inspector accepting that none of us had been anywhere near Jacques at the time in question so our interviews were very short.

On the way to our room we slowed in response to raised voices coming from Julien and Genevieve's room. Julien was ranting about someone telling the Inspector about a heated conversation he'd had with Jacques.

'Why would they do that?' Genevieve demanded.

'To make trouble!' Snarled Julien.

'But you did speak to him,' insisted Genevieve.

'He was going on about his fishing license that's all.'

'And what about the doctor? I saw you talking to him, and he looked uncomfortable. What was that about?' Genevieve said accusingly.

'Bah! Jacques also got stroppy with the doctor, demanding he help him get the fishing license. The doctor came to me to ask if there was anything I could do but I told him I couldn't and that was all!'
'You're sure there was nothing else because I don't want to be dragged into this…If you're hiding something!'
'Stop nagging! There's nothing more to it!'
It went quiet suddenly then the doorknob rattled before someone pulled open the door. Startled, we hurriedly continued on our way, desperate not to be caught skulking.
Once in our room we breathed a group sigh of relief and collapsed onto our beds.
'Well now we know why Celia thought there was a heated discussion between Jacques and the doctor,' said Di
'Yeah, he seems to have been asking everyone to help get him the fishing license.' I replied.
'There doesn't seem to be any motive for killing Jacques though,' said Marie.
Di and I agreed.
'Maybe the Inspector's right and it was an accident after all.' Mused Di.

We'd been told that Collette wouldn't be around the rest of the day, so Marie and Di offered to walk to a nearby *boulangerie* to buy sandwiches for our lunch and allow me some privacy for my WhatsApp call to Karl.
Karl and I hadn't spoken since the day I'd left for our trip so we spent time chatting about Geraldine, her family and Ruffec. Knowing Karl would be uneasy knowing I was in the company of a potential murderer I tried to be, shall we say, economical with the truth. I therefore told him about Jacques' tragic accident leading to his death and how Geraldine's family were there for the reading of her

husband's will. Finally he asked me if I'd had the chance to give his news some thought. I hesitated, thinking about how events since our arrival had kept my mind occupied.

Karl noticed my hesitation and smiled. 'We can discuss it when I get back if you like, there's no rush.'

I returned his smile and was about to ask him if he knew exactly what day he'd be back when Marie and Di burst into the room.

Chatting and laughing they halted immediately when they saw I was still on my call.

'It's okay, I'm just about finished.' I grinned at them.

Di mouthed 'sorry' with a pained look.

I looked back at Karl. 'Di and Marie are back, so…'

He grinned and waved at the camera as I turned the laptop so he could see them. They waved in return, calling hello then goodbye.

Karl still grinning good naturedly said he would be in touch later in the week before ending the call. Afterwards, neither Di nor Marie made any attempt to discover anything about our future plans, so I made no mention of it.

CHAPTER NINE

We'd agreed to meet up with Sophie and Lesley at the evening market
so we left the manor around seven to begin our walk into town.

Noticing Marie pause at the gate to peer at several cars parked on the other side of the road, Di and I followed suit, waiting expectantly for an explanation.

'When we popped out earlier to get bread, you know for lunch? I was sure I caught a glimpse of Inspector Maupetit with one of his officers sitting in a car across there.' She nodded faintly toward the cars.

'Maybe I'm being paranoid but it looked like they were watching this house.'
'Hm why would they do that?' Asked Di.
'He didn't notice you?' I asked, ignoring Di's question.
She grinned. '*Eh bien*, you know I think he may have because it looked as if he slid down in his seat, you know as if he was trying not to be seen.'
Both Di and I giggled.
'So not expecting someone to recognise him then.' Said Di.
'Subtle.' I remarked.

We met Sophie and Lesley outside the church on the second and final evening of their trip to stroll leisurely around the market stalls which were placed around the edge of the main square. Stopping now and again, we admired the wares, stopping for several minutes to watch, among other things, a sculptor carving small wooden animal figurines. At a stall manned by local winemakers, we stopped for a little winetasting before Lesley bought two bottles. Sophie declaring an interest in the handmade jewellery items for sale, ended up buying a pair of amber earrings.
When Lesley proclaimed her hunger, we agreed to stop for a bite to eat and opted to buy galettes, taking seats at one of the long trestle tables temporarily set up to encourage dining from the various food stalls. Marie went astray for several minutes after we sat down but reappeared holding two rather large carafes of red wine and a bag containing several plastic glasses.
The evening air was cool but we were warmed by the food, drinks and convivial atmosphere. With the market being busy, the breeze was lessened by people toing and froing nearby and strings of lights overhead, which came on as daylight faded, seemed to increase the

warmth of the evening. With all thoughts of Geraldine's worries for the time being put out of mind, we spent our time chatting and laughing together.

There was a brief lull in the conversation when Di surprised us by saying she'd just noticed Julien leave the restaurant directly opposite. We all turned to peer in that direction but were too late to catch a glimpse of him. Marie and I however, were quick to spot one of the Inspector's officers emerge from the shadows at the side of the same restaurant and head toward the market entrance. We glanced at each other to register our surprise before turning our attention immediately back to the officer, discovering that he appeared to be following Julien, who was now well ahead of him among a crowd of market visitors. When Julien disappeared into one of the bars, the officer pulled back to stand in the shadows which coincidentally happened to be near our table. Sensing our stares, he peered at us curiously but shrunk further into the gloom, reluctant to admit that he'd been discovered. Refusing to ignore him, we continued to gaze at him openly, causing him to struggle with the decision of whether to leave his hideout or stay put. Deciding on the latter, he maintained his position but continued to throw wary looks in our direction.

'Come and join us,' blurted Lesley.

Now looking stricken, no doubt believing we'd blown his cover, he didn't respond.

'We'll see him if he leaves the bar so you can follow him once again.' Coaxed Marie as she pushed her hair back and fluttered her eyelashes. The rest of us traded amused glances at Marie's open flirting which after only a moment's hesitation persuaded the policeman to move forward into the light.

'So you're part of this operation?' His voice low, he directed his question at me.

I gave him a quizzical look.

'Madame Patterson *n'est pas*?' He asked.
Wondering what was going on but not wanting to reveal our ignorance I pretended to have a clue what he was talking about so nodded confidently in response to both questions. Catching a glimpse of the others nudging each other and hearing Lesley giggle made him glance at the others suspiciously.
'Well, yes the operation,' I repeated slowly and sighed. 'Inspector Maupetit speaks so fast sometimes I can't catch everything he says so I need to check with him for the exact location.'
He looked guarded. 'Yes better that he tells you the details.'
I nodded, feeling thwarted. We clearly had our work cut out encouraging him to take us into his confidence. Marie, having had the same thought, tried again to work her magic.
'Why not sit down and have a drink while you wait for Julien to leave the bar.' She flashed a dazzling smile. 'No sense in one pair of eyes watching when we can all help.'
Overcome by temptation, he agreed that five pair of eyes was better than one and took a seat at the table. Conscious that Marie had successfully lured the young officer into our lair, we all shared a sly grin. Sophie placed a wine glass in front of him and Marie poured wine into it. 'If I know Inspector Maupetit, I'm sure he won't mind you having a break.'
The officer was about to protest the amount of wine was too much when Sophie picked it up and pushed it into his hand. Looking bemused suddenly that five women were giving him so much attention, he smiled nervously and took a large gulp.
Losing no time, we clinked our glasses with his while wishing him good health.
'*Santé*!' We chorused.
Too polite to refuse he took another sip.

Deciding it was going to take a while to get information out of him if he was only taking small sips meant we needed to up our game. I raised a toast.

'To helping officers of the law,' I said brightly and clinked his glass again. He smiled uncertainly but took another sip. Guessing what I was up to, the others began to raise toasts of their own.

'To helping each other,' said Lesley and moved to clink glasses again as we all did.

'To catching criminals,' said Di. He took another drink.

Marie smiled at him, gazing into his eyes. 'Of course, we all know Didier, your Inspector. I can tell you he will be very pleased that you've enlisted our help with Julien.'

The officer, responded by insisting we call him Théo, and agreeing that he had no doubt the Inspector would be impressed that he'd managed to find people who could help him with his surveillance, especially those already involved in the operation.

'It must be exhausting having to wait while watching for someone to come in and out of restaurants and other places,' I ventured.

'Mm,' nodded Théo agreeing, 'It isn't the most interesting part of the job.'

'How long are you expecting Julien to be in there?'

Théo looked uncertain again.

'I mean knowing what he's up to, you must have some idea, as you're so much more knowledgeable than we are about these things,' I said, playing to his ego.

He immediately looked pleased with himself. '*Tout à fait*, we, er don't think the others are around, but of course he's in contact with them.'

'Oh yes of course, I agree,' I nodded enthusiastically.

I sensed the others glancing at each other in confusion and willed them not to give the game away just as Théo said 'but it's only a few places in this town so far.'

'Mm what makes you think that, would you say?' I asked, still no clearer about what we were discussing.

He frowned suddenly and I wondered if he was beginning to suspect I didn't know anything. Time to ply him with more drink.

Marie, with the same thought, topped up his wine. Di clinked her glass with his again. 'To successful endeavours.'

To our delight he took a rather large gulp.

'So the operation…' I said thoughtfully.

He nodded and grinned. 'Should be over by tonight if they all turn up.'

'*Tu sais*, I'm trying to think exactly, how long it would take to get there,' Marie smiled sweetly at him before picking up her phone. 'I should put the address in to check, er, now what was it again?' She added as if to herself.

'*Pas loin*, not far, so shouldn't take long.' He said before taking another gulp but still without disclosing the exact location.

'You're expecting Julien to show up of course,' I said.

'*Bien sur*'

I looked at my watch absently 'So we've still got er …'

'Three hours,' he said obligingly, finishing off the wine in his glass.

Marie topped it up again.

'Of course, yes,' I replied.

'You think the Inspector will arrest Julien?' Asked Sophie who sat on one side of Théo and pushed his wine glass now on the table toward his hand once again.

'Oh no doubt!' Replied Théo enthusiastically.

Fortunately Théo still seemed oblivious to our confused expressions because of his focus on the bar opposite and now that he was enjoying the wine without our encouragement.

I pondered what we'd managed to glean from him: the Inspector was after Julien, and it seemed he was supposed to be ambushing him in some type of operation in three hours' time. Of course, we still didn't know where this would take place and what it was he was accused of. To fill in the gaps I was about to ask Théo outright what Julien was up to in the hope that the alcohol had left him more open to answering our direct questions. Unfortunately, it was at that moment that he spied Julien. Excusing himself from our company Théo stood up without any sign of inebriation, though his eyes were looking decidedly glassy. We watched him leave, moving through the tightly packed crowd in pursuit of Julien with a little more clumsiness than we'd previously witnessed. Seeing him being forced to apologise several times after stumbling into people meant the wine had taken affect and I felt a little guilty about our behaviour, guessing the Inspector would not react well to having one of his officers drunk on duty.

CHAPTER TEN

It was around eleven thirty when Sophie and Lesley returned to their hotel and we made our way back to the house. On entering our room we discovered a note had been pushed under the door. It was addressed to Marie and stated simply 'midnight in the boat house – information to your advantage. Come alone'.
Since it was just after twelve, it was too late to comply with the conditions of the invitation but Marie still decided to go. She reasoned that the person who'd sent the note might still be hanging around.
'We can't let you go alone, it's too dangerous.' Said Di.
'We'll stay well back, and you can go in on your own but we'll be right outside.' I added.
With no time to argue Marie conceded.
The light from the full moon in the clear night sky helped us to pick our way through the grounds. This was just as well since none of us had had the foresight to bring a torch. Once the boathouse was in sight

we automatically quickened our pace before slowing to a creep as we grew close. Without a thought for her own safety Marie marched straight in while we remained outside as agreed.

Seconds later, a shriek from Marie spurred us to action and we rushed inside to her rescue. Straining my eyes to try to see through the pitch black of the room was useless so I gave all my attention to listening intently for any sound.

'Marie?' I whispered, sensing Di close behind.

As my eyes adjusted to the gloom, I gasped. A tall shadowy figure was slowly crossing my path. Frozen in fright, I tried hard to identify the person just as a whimpering sound came from my left. Feeling sure Marie was in danger I felt around for an object to use as a weapon. Unfortunately, my hand brushed roughly against the edge of a nearby table causing something to tumble and crash to the floor. Expecting the figure to react violently to the noise, I frantically felt around the same area with both hands. Distinguishing an object as a glass bottle, I grasped hold of the neck, intending to use it as a weapon. At that same moment, Marie screamed as the shadowy figure lunged in her direction. With my heart in my mouth and still limited vision, I moved cautiously toward them.

Suddenly, the whole place was flooded with light. Blinking to adjust my eyes, I felt Di bump into me, her hand tightly clutching my arm. Marie sat on the floor holding a blood-stained knife. A man lay prone and very still beside her.

My mouth dropped open in shock while I stood rooted to the floor in stunned silence. Marie, suddenly registering the knife in her hand, recoiled and released her grip as if it was on fire. Then, as if from nowhere, Inspector Maupetit rushed forward to turn the man over, looking for any vital life signs.

'Julien!' Gasped Di.

The Inspector stood up just as Julien's lifeless body was surrounded by several officers who were crowding into the boat house. Taking in the scene the Inspector turned slowly to gaze from Marie to me and Di in astonishment. Realising at that precise moment that I was holding a wine bottle aloft as if to strike someone, I hastily lowered my arm.

The Inspector remained tight lipped while one of his officers moved toward Marie with handcuffs.

Marie shook her head, her eyes wide with fear. 'It wasn't…I didn't.'

The Inspector ignored her protests and nodded at another officer who picked up the knife and placed it into an evidence bag.

'I'll take that *s'il vous plait.*'

Numb, I gaped as an officer appeared in front of me holding out his hand for the wine bottle. I passed it to him automatically, puzzled as to what I was even doing with it.

'Evidence.' The Inspector's no-nonsense voice jolted me back to reality.

I watched in a daze as Marie, her hands in cuffs behind her back, passed by, escorted out of the boat house by an officer.

I finally found my voice. 'You can't be serious Inspector! Marie wouldn't…'

'Why are you all here?' The Inspector cut me off, his expression had changed from being stunned to being livid.

Di and I started talking simultaneously.

'A note was pushed under our bedroom door,' explained Di.

'We thought there might be some information to do with Jacques.' I added.

'We had to follow Marie as we didn't think it would be safe for her to meet someone alone.'

'She certainly had no reason *at all* to kill Julien.'

'Two people dead now – that's of course if Jacques was even murdered.' Di gazed at me.

Shaking his head in bewilderment, the Inspector held up his hand to halt our words before closing his eyes despairingly and breathing a heavy sigh. 'Jacques?'
Unintentionally we both started talking over the top of each other again.
The Inspector shook his head, his face stony. '*S'il vous plaît!* Please leave so my officers can secure this crime scene. I will question you both tomorrow.'
He turned his back on us then which immediately made my hackles rise.
'But you can't arrest Marie. She didn't kill him!'
The Inspector paused and looked down at Julien's body thoughtfully before turning around slowly to study my face. He spoke slowly and with forced calm.
'Caught holding what appeared to be the murder weapon, I have no option but to take Madame Reynard in for questioning. If I allowed her to leave the crime scene when she is clearly the prime suspect, I would not be doing my job. You of all people should appreciate that *Madame Patterson.*'
'But…' I protested instinctively.
The Inspector flashed me a warning look. 'Of course, you both could be arrested now as accessories.'
I flushed, searching for a retort but Di pulled at my arm.
'C'mon Catherine,' she urged.
Taking one last glance at the body, my mind whirled with questions so I opened my mouth in one last attempt, but the Inspector had already turned away, determined to brook no argument. Finally feeling helpless, I heeded Di's advice.

CHAPTER ELEVEN

News of Julien's death spread fast among the household with everyone appearing in a state of shock. The doctor arrived early that morning to administer Geraldine with medication to calm her nerves and advised complete bed rest while Irène ensured everyone knew that Geraldine was not to be disturbed under any circumstances.

The police were expected to arrive at some point before noon to question everyone but having already arranged to meet Sophie and Lesley for breakfast and despite Marie still being in custody, Di and I decided to stick to our plans. Besides, we both felt it was more appropriate to allow time for the rest of the family to begin grieving without outsiders in their midst.

So, although we knew we'd incur the Inspector's wrath due to our absence, we left the house.

Having just passed through the gates on leaving the property we were surprised to come across Genevieve pacing up and down on the pavement outside. A cigarette between her fingers and a strained expression, she glanced at us briefly before averting her eyes. Finding her actions suspicious, we approached her warily.

'Waiting for a taxi,' she replied to our questioning looks.

'But won't the police want to question you?' I asked gently, trying to show some compassion.

She took several furious puffs from her cigarette, her hand shaking, betraying her frayed nerves. She shook her head. 'Not taking any chances, need to get somewhere safe.'

'What do you mean?' I asked, but she was too distracted to respond. When the taxi pulled up next to her, she immediately dropped the cigarette, extinguished it with her foot and picked up a small holdall from the pavement. Then, leaping into the taxi and without a backward glance, she was gone. Watching the car disappear into the distance Di gave me a bemused look. 'What on earth is going on?'

I shook my head. 'I have absolutely no idea!'

*

Sophie and Lesley were already sitting at the table when we arrived at the bistro. They were equally appalled to hear what had happened the previous night and especially that our friend had been arrested on suspicion of murder.

With Marie dominating our thoughts, we discussed our frustration at her arrest and resolved to find ways we could help prove her innocence. As a result, both Sophie and Lesley offered to extend their stay at the hotel to help but we assured them there was nothing they could do as we didn't know ourselves what was going on. Reluctantly they agreed that they would only stay for the time already planned and wished us luck, insisting we keep them informed of our progress. Since none of us felt we could enjoy breakfast while Marie was being held in a cell, we spent only a short while together after ordering coffee and a *pain au raisin* each, merely to assuage our hunger.

*

When Di and I arrived back at the house the interviews were in full swing. Luckily we had not been missed. Some family members had made it their business to report to the police that Genevieve had hastily left the house that morning to get a taxi, so as far as everyone in the house was concerned, she was almost certainly involved in Julien's death, if not guilty of his actual murder.

Collette however had a different story to tell. Wanting some insight into how the interviews were going but not feeling sufficiently comfortable enough to ask family members, I went into the kitchen with the premise of being desperate for a cup of tea. I found Collette putting away dishes. She immediately offered to make the tea, saying she would be glad of the distraction as recent events were causing her too much stress. I sympathised and confided that I was concerned for Marie's welfare seeing as she had been arrested as the main suspect for Julien's murder despite me knowing her to be innocent. I repeated the family's belief that Genevieve was the culprit and said I wondered whether it could be true.

Collette shook her head vehemently.

'I sat last night with Gen talking for hours.'

I was struck by her use of the shortened, more familiar name.

'It turns out we came from the same small village, years apart of course but we chatted as if we were old friends. She mentioned she was having trouble sleeping so I gave her one of her one of my sleeping pills around eleven. Now they really knock you out. Anyway, I went in to check on her just before twelve and she was fast asleep. No way on earth she could have left the house to murder anybody.'

'And she didn't mention where Julien had gone yesterday evening?'

Again she shook her head. 'Never really discussed him. I got the feeling she didn't want to know where he was or what he was up to really.'

'And you told all this to the Inspector?' I asked, concerned that if Genevieve wasn't the murderer then Marie must still be in the frame.

'Oh yes, he knows. Though why she left before talking to the police is anyone's guess. I mean I can see that it makes her look rather guilty.'

Just then Di entered the kitchen and looked at me. 'You've been summoned. I've just been in, told him the same thing as we did last night.' She smiled wryly.

I sighed and stood up wearily, dreading the third degree.

'Though he seems in a better mood than he was then.' Added Di. 'Oh and by the way, he said Marie was released in the early hours of this morning.'

I beamed a smile feeling pleased but confused. 'Early hours? So where is she?'

Di shrugged. 'I sent her a text as soon as I found out and she replied that she's ok, not to worry and we'll see her later.'

Nonplussed I shook my head wondering what she was up to.

I walked into the dining room to find the Inspector seated at the table next to Théo, the officer we had plied with drinks the previous evening. The officer averted his eyes whereas the Inspector gave me a direct look and instructed me to sit down. He glanced at the officer.
'I believe you and Sergeant Laurent are already acquainted,' he said the drily. The officer reddened.
'Yes, we've met,' I replied innocently.
The Inspector studied my face for several moments then turned to the sergeant who was sitting poised ready to take notes of the conversation. 'I will take it from here Sergeant.'
The officer looked up in surprise '*Mais…*'
The Inspector gave him a dark look.
'*Bien sur,*' he hurriedly put down his pen and closed the notebook before pushing his seat back and standing up. He then glanced briefly at me before hurrying for the door.
I braced myself for the onslaught which came almost immediately.
'You made no mention of why you were here when we met at the restaurant,' the Inspector began in a rather stern tone.
'I might say the same of you.' I retorted, reminded that he'd knowingly given the impression that he was in the area to meet up with old friends.
He looked taken aback. 'I do not make it my business to keep members of the public informed of my work.'
'And I have no reason to inform a policeman about anything I'm doing.' I snapped.
An irritated look flashed across his face but he didn't respond while I seethed with indignation. The ensuing silence of what felt like several minutes became uncomfortable and I wondered if we had anything further to say to each other.
Finally the Inspector sighed and said in a conciliatory tone. 'I understand you are here to visit Madame Geraldine.'

I met his eyes with a defiant look and was deliberately slow to reply. 'I am, what of it?'

He looked down at his notes and seemed to be struggling with his thoughts. Finally he met my gaze and choosing his words carefully he said, 'I've been informed by Madame Harley that your hostess has some concerns about her safety. I would like to know what your thoughts are on this.'

I stared at him in stunned silence. Was he asking for my opinion about Geraldine's concerns, or did he just want to know what I'd found out about the threat to her life?

'Madame?' He prompted.

Relenting, I cleared my throat and moved to sit more comfortably in the chair.

'Well, first of all, I'm not sure Geraldine's concerns are genuine. She believes that her life is in danger from someone in the family but we, er, *I* have not witnessed any antagonism toward her from them.'

The Inspector waited patiently for me to continue, giving me his full attention. Used to him being more dismissive of my opinions, I found his interest a little disconcerting.

'Secondly Jacques, the fisherman, Malarie's father?'

He nodded, frowning.

'Well, Geraldine told us he knew about the threatening note which had been left with her dead cat, a cat that had been poisoned and which Jacques had confirmed because he was a vet, but then he denied knowing anything about it and so we're starting to think Geraldine's confused. And then Jacques died. An experienced fisherman simply slipped and fell into the lake - which Malarie doesn't believe by the way. Of course Inspector Borné agreed to question everyone only after Malarie kicked up a fuss as he was keen to dismiss the death as an accident without any further investigation.'

The Inspector narrowed his eyes, searching my face. 'And you believe his death to be suspicious?'

I shrugged. 'The note, the poisoned cat, him denying all knowledge of it. Seemed strange that's all.'

The Inspector nodded slowly and sighed resignedly, clearly not convinced. 'Tell me how you came to be in the boat house with the others when Julien was murdered.'

'We went into town for the evening market.'

'Yes,' he raised an eyebrow and gave me a knowing look. 'I have a witness who can corroborate that.'

I reddened and avoided his gaze, thinking about how we'd coerced his sergeant into revealing some, though not all, information.

'We told you the rest last night.'

He nodded. 'Indulge me. Tell me again.'

I sighed. 'When we returned just after twelve, we found a note had been slipped under the door addressed to Marie, saying to meet at twelve in the boathouse for information to her advantage. Because it was already after twelve, we hurried there in the hope that the person hadn't already left.'

'So you weren't surprised it was addressed to Marie?'

I shook my head choosing my words carefully. 'We just thought it was something to do with Geraldine, and as Marie is a close family friend, it didn't seem unusual.'

'I see,' he was watching me closely.

'Then you know the rest, she went in and we stayed outside but then when she screamed, we ran in to try to help her.'

The Inspector nodded but looked cynical. 'And that's all?'

I shrugged. 'I don't know anything else.'

He studied me for a few moments and was about to speak but then thought better of it.

'Ok you may go.' He said simply, taking his attention to his notebook.

*

After my dismissal I returned to our room to find Marie and Di sitting enjoying a cup of tea.

'Thank goodness!' I beamed. We embraced warmly.

'Was it awful?' I asked, concerned.

She shook her head. 'I wasn't put in a cell or anything. I made a statement explaining what happened then they let me go.'

'And how you came to be holding murder weapon?' Prompted Di.

Marie shrugged. 'I explained that I fell backwards onto the floor when Julien stumbled into me. I put my hands onto the floor to push myself up, not knowing Julien was dead and put my hand straight onto the knife. I didn't realise what it was in the dark so when the light came on, I panicked and dropped it, especially when I saw the body on the floor next to me.'

'So where have you been since they released you?' I asked.

'I went to meet Hugo and we stayed up the rest of the night talking,' she yawned and stretched her arms as if to prove what she'd said was true.

I was still puzzled. 'And?'

'When I was questioned at the police station, I was asked several times whether I'd been in touch with Hugo. They wouldn't say why they wanted to know. Then, when I left the station at around two this morning, I found a text on my phone from Hugo asking me to meet him urgently. So, wondering about the content of his text and the police' questions about Hugo, I decided that somehow there must be a connection. *Alors*, I phoned him there and then and he answered immediately asking me to meet him straightaway.'

She paused to drink her tea and rubbed her eyes.

I glanced at Di who was looking baffled but waiting patiently for more.

'Anyway,' continued Marie with another yawn, 'he wanted to know what had happened to Julien.'

'He knew him?'

She shrugged. 'He was agitated, shocked that Julien had been killed but reluctant to tell me more.'

'So what was his urgency then?'

Marie lay down on the bed. 'He wanted to know if anyone had been at the house asking for him and wanting to know where he was.'

'Why would someone come here looking for Hugo?'

Marie closed her eyes and yawned again. 'All he would say was that he had some business dealings with Julien and that they had turned sour. He said that he had to be careful about who he could trust.'

I opened my mouth to question her further but from the sound of her breathing she was now fast asleep.

Di moved to pull a cover over Marie and we sat drinking our tea in silence for a few minutes.

'I wonder what business Hugo had with Julien?' I whispered.

Di shook her head, 'curiouser and curiouser,' she muttered.

Deciding we'd be better leaving Marie alone, we picked up our coats and headed downstairs.

CHAPTER TWELVE

It was another mild October day and the sun was shining. We took the path bordering the flower beds while admiring the variety of colour still present so late in the season. When we reached the lake we stopped to gaze around, deliberately avoiding the area where Jacques had been found. 'I'm guessing that's the gardener.' Di gestured toward a man pushing a wheelbarrow on the other side of the lake.

I laughed lightly, 'Hm, what gave him away?'

'Was he questioned about Jacques' death?' Asked Di.

I nodded. 'I heard when the interviews with Inspector Borné were being held that Aldert wasn't needed as the day Jacques died was usually his day off.'

Di nodded and we fell silent, our minds returning once again to the recent deaths. Minutes later and unable to stop ourselves from discussing them, we took turns reiterating the facts as if something obvious was going to jump out at us.

'Jacques may or may not have been killed deliberately.' I pointed out.

Di nodded, 'And Julien was murdered but we don't know why.'

I watched Aldert stop to inspect one of the shrubs. 'Genevieve, though her leaving early was suspicious, had a cast iron alibi from Collette.'

'And she was scared.' Added Di.

'Oh yes definitely. But what part is Hugo playing in this?'

Di followed my gaze to watch Aldert. 'And why was Julien going from restaurant to restaurant?'

'And being followed by the police.' I narrowed my eyes thoughtfully.

'Is Julien's death in any way connected to Jacques' death?' Di said almost to herself. 'So many questions.' She mused then turned to look directly at me. 'We need to discover why Julien was being followed.'

I shrugged. 'I agree. But I'm not sure how I could inveigle my way into finding that out from the Inspector.'

Deciding to go back into the house via the conservatory we were surprised to find Geraldine sitting at the table, writing in her notebook. Unable to pass up an opportunity to question her and despite her grief, we lingered after greeting her.

'Have you found something?' She enquired; her expression weary.

'No,' I shook my head, feeling guilty for our lack of progress. 'We were hoping you might be able shed some light on the reason for Julien…' I left the rest unsaid.

She shook her head, 'Inspector Maupetit has already questioned me about this, and I couldn't tell him anything either.'

'So you don't know of anything he was involved in which may have put him in harm's way?' I asked gently.

She sighed and her hand went to her forehead 'I, I should have come clean about it all.'

Di and I shared a puzzled glance.

'What do you mean?' I prompted gently.

At that moment the door opened as if someone had entered the room from the house. We all turned to look but strangely, no one appeared. Ignoring the interruption I persisted. 'Are you saying you know something which could help find Julien's killer?'

Geraldine frowned, looking down at her notes. I shot Di a hopeful sideways glance, anticipating an explanation from Geraldine. Unfortunately, Geraldine avoided my question. 'My head is aching. I think I need to rest now.'

'Of course,' I said trying not to be too disappointed.

Di and I interweaved our way between several large potted plants which screened the door to find the doctor gazing down at the screen on his phone.

'*Bonjour,*' said Di cheerily to the top of his head as we passed. Without acknowledging our presence he simply started toward Geraldine.

I gave Di a meaningful look to signify what I thought of his rudeness before loitering after opening the door, just long enough to hear him tell Geraldine that he needed to answer a phone call. We then heard the outside door open and close and assumed he'd gone into the garden for some privacy.

Collette was in the kitchen when we sauntered in.

'Oh, Catherine,' she said, turning to look at me as she wiped a cloth over a countertop. 'Inspector Maupetit just telephoned to ask if you could meet him.'

'Oh?' I frowned. Had he thought of something else he needed to question me about?
'The *Jardin de la rose* at three o'clock this afternoon.'
Di and I exchanged surprised looks before heading out into the garden. I checked my watch. 'Ooh, I'd better get a move on then.'
'See you later.' Said Di as she headed back upstairs.

After a brisk walk into town I arrived early at the *Jardin de la rose* after discovering the entrance on the *rue de la chaine.* Wandering around the rose beds with no one else around felt very peaceful and I took the time alone to enjoy the beauty and fragrance of the flowers. Bending at one point to smell a gorgeous yellow rose I got a sense that someone was hovering behind me. Just as I was about to turn around I caught a glimpse of the Inspector striding past the entrance. Surprised that he seemed to be heading in the wrong direction to meet me, I moved quickly to intercept him. Unfortunately he was too far ahead, so quickening my pace I followed him across the main road toward a café opposite. It occurred to me that the message I'd received to meet him must have been lost in translation as he seemed to have no intention of a *rendezvous* in the rose garden.
The Inspector took a seat at a table and moments later I collapsed down into the seat opposite. He gazed at me in astonishment.
'Not expecting me so soon?' I grinned, catching my breath.
He raised his eyebrows. 'Not expecting you at all.'
'What? But your message,' I started, looking at him in confusion.
'Message Madame?' He shook his head looking dumbfounded, 'not from me.'
'I don't understand,' I frowned, recalling the message from Collette who'd taken his call.
'Someone is playing a trick on you I think.' He offered.
'Why would...?' I began, feeling anxious as to a possible reason.

He shook his head and shrugged off any misunderstanding 'Since you're here, would you like coffee?'

I stared at him without seeing, still feeling confused. 'But I was supposed to meet you in the rose garden, at least that was the message, and coincidentally you're here, only steps away.'

He shrugged. 'Coincidence, as you say.'

'Is it?' I asked in disbelief.

He shrugged again. 'Did you go there? Was there someone there perhaps that you knew?'

I began to feel uneasy. 'Actually I was in there alone until I saw you walk past the entrance but…'

The Inspector waited patiently for me to continue.

'…I heard, no, I *sensed*, that someone else was in there with me just before I left.'

The Inspector searched my face.

'I didn't see who it was.' I said, predicting his next question.

The Inspector nodded and lifted a hand to catch the attention of the waiter who arrived promptly at our table. 'Would you like something stronger *Madame*?'

I stared at him uncomprehending. Someone had sent a message for me to meet them. Could that person have been in the rose garden with me with the intention of doing me harm? I had to consider it was a real possibility.

'Madame Patterson?' The Inspector repeated as the waiter hovered.

I took a deep breath and forced a smile, trying to recover some composure. 'No, no coffee's fine.'

The Inspector nodded and the waiter left.

I glanced around, suddenly seeing the café and its diners as if for the first time. The Inspector remained silent, watching my stricken face and waiting patiently for me to calm down. Sitting forward suddenly, I gave him a serious look. 'I had intended to ask why you needed to speak to me.'

The waiter returned to place our coffees on the table so I waited until he left before resuming.

'But now I know it wasn't actually you…'

The Inspector shrugged again. Looking unconcerned he pulled his cup toward him before taking a sip.

'Since you are here perhaps we can share some information.'

I sighed and gave a wry smile. 'I'm guessing you need more information from me than you are willing to give.'

The Inspector looked affronted. 'It is the nature of my job…'

'I know, I know, you're not going to tell any Tom, Dick or Harry what's going on in your investigations.' I interrupted irritably.

'Tom, Dick or …?'

I waved a dismissive hand, sighing. 'Oh, never mind. What is it you want to know?'

He stared at me thoughtfully for several moments then as if coming to a decision he sat forward, resting his arms on the table and lowering his voice confidentially. Unexpectedly, he began to explain the circumstances surrounding his visit to Ruffec. Sitting upright I gave him all my attention while gazing at him with increasing disbelief as he described how Julien and perhaps Genevieve as well, were involved in a scam selling cheap Spanish wine and relabelling it as expensive French wine before selling it on to restaurants and cafés.

When he was finished I leaned back in my seat digesting his words. 'And is Hugo also involved in this?'

The Inspector sighed and gazed into the middle distance as if struggling with how much more to disclose.

'Marie told me you questioned her about Hugo.' I persisted.

The Inspector sat tight lipped for a few more minutes while considering my words. Finally, his face took on a resigned look but he was still slow to respond. 'Hugo bought some of the wine without realising.' He shrugged and gave me a meaningful look.

'*Malheureusement*, he can be gullible. Anyway, he was duped because the taster he was given was actually decent wine. But when he started to get a few of the more discerning customers complaining about it, he guessed what Julien and his team were up to. He confronted Julien but found himself being threatened.'

I sat forward again, all ears.

'Hugo has been in trouble with the law before and the scammers were keen to have him look as guilty as they were if he went to the authorities.'

'Yet he came to you?'

The Inspector looked uncomfortable and shifted in his seat. 'We go way back, old er, acquaintances, you might say. He knew he could trust me with the information even if I couldn't act on it.'

I looked at him in amazement. 'So I'm guessing you were prepared to keep him out of it.'

He tilted his head. 'I told him I would keep him out of it if he set up a meeting with Julien and one or more of his contacts or suppliers. The idea was that a meeting would be arranged so we could catch them in making the transactions, you know, exchanging money or wine. We would find out who the actors in the scam were and could possibly catch them with some of the evidence. We would be there of course to surprise them and make the arrests at the meeting.'

'So that was the meeting at the boat house.' I realised now why the policeman had been so keen to take the bottle of wine from my hand.

'*Oui*, but then three women turned up and Julien was murdered.' He added drily.

I pulled a face. 'I have already explained about the note Marie received.'

The Inspector raised his hands in surrender. '*Oui, oui*, it has all been explained.' He gave me a look of mock irritation. 'Though I cannot say I'm happy about how you coaxed my sergeant into supplying you with information.'

I grinned. 'I do hope we didn't get him into too much trouble.'

The Inspector smiled wryly and shook his head without comment. Clearly not angry, I wondered if he was mellowing.

'And what about Genevieve?' I asked, taking a more serious note.

'My guess is that she is in hiding. Perhaps concerned that whoever killed Julien will come after her, if she is also part of this scam, which we do not know yet for sure.'

I nodded, 'yes, fearful for her own life would make sense. She was very nervous when we came across her waiting for a taxi. But what I find hard to understand is, can Julien really have been murdered over a few cases of wine?'

The Inspector shook his head. 'Not a few cases Madame. This is a large operation, involving hundreds of thousands, if not millions of euros, not to mention the genuine vineyard owners who are missing out on their usual revenue for their own fine wines, so livelihoods are also at stake...'

I interrupted his soliloquy, trying to bring him back to the matter at hand. 'Yes, yes, okay, I see what you mean. So you believe it's one of the scammers, his contacts, that killed Julien?'

Indignant at being interrupted he shrugged and looked away. 'Perhaps but we are still looking into it.'

'I suppose if the scammers thought they were being set up by Julien it could be a motive for his murder, but why would they suspect Julien had set them up? I mean wasn't it Hugo who instigated the meeting? Wasn't Julien kept in the dark?'

The Inspector gave me a sharp look. 'As far as we know, *oui*, Julien was unaware of the set up so his murder for that reason doesn't make sense. No one would suspect Julien.'

'Unless Hugo tipped them off?' Had the Inspector considered other possibilities despite their friendship.

The Inspector raised his eyebrows at my suggestion. 'What we do know is that one of Julien's contacts, a Spaniard we had under surveillance who was, we believe, travelling to the meeting, telephoned for assistance when his car broke down. He was taken to the nearest village eighty kilometres away, so he has an alibi for that night. He was the only one we knew about but we know there are many others in the network.'

'So you're no closer to finding out who killed Julien or why.' I mused. The Inspector shook his head slowly, looking thoughtful.

Just then his phone rang. After only a few brief words the call was over. With a look of relief the Inspector glanced at his watch then summoned the waiter. He beamed a smile. 'As I am not needed for at least another hour and I'm off duty for the rest of the day, would you like to join me in a glass of wine?'

My instinct was to immediately refuse. 'Why not?' I returned his smile suddenly wondering why I'd agreed.

We sipped our wine for a few minutes in silence before I decided, in the spirit of cooperation, to explain fully why I was a guest at Geraldine's house.

I reminded him that Geraldine was convinced someone in the family meant to bring her harm and together with Marie and Di, we were supposed to be finding out which one it was.

'The problem is that I'm finding the family, her children, to be pleasant, well, with the exception of Julien but then he's out of the picture now anyway.' I paused hoping I hadn't sounded too callous and took a sip of wine.

The Inspector looked confused by my comment for a moment before his face cleared. 'She has given reasons why she believes her life to be to be threatened?'

'Well, if you remember I told you she said her cat was poisoned and there was a note with it, as if it was deliberate but she can't remember exactly what it said, nor what happened to it. Also it seems to be impossible to find anyone to corroborate her story.'

The Inspector frowned but remained silent.

'She is very ill of course so drugs may be causing her confusion. And now to add to her stress is Julien's death, especially as she had only recently told him that his biological father wasn't her husband, well, the husband everyone believed she had.'

The Inspector was now looking baffled.

I waved a dismissive hand. 'Oh, long story. Anyway, Julien reacted by becoming rather distraught, maybe even angry. I suppose that must make Geraldine feel terrible, you know causing her son emotional pain not long before he died.'

'When did she tell him exactly?'

I recalled Genevieve asking about Julien's whereabouts while he was in with Geraldine.

'The day Jacques was found. Julien left Geraldine to go into the garden a short time before. And you know Julien and Genevieve were very snippy with each other, not that that has anything to do with it I suppose.'

The Inspector nodded and suggested that maybe they were more like business partners than romantically involved despite their engagement. I nodded, agreeing it was a possibility. I also broached the subject of Jacques death and how Malarie believed it wasn't an accident.

'Yes, you mentioned that before. But why does she suspect murder? Does she know of any motive?'

I shook my head. 'I just know Malarie is adamant that it wasn't an accident. And I suppose the fact that Julien was in the garden puts him in the vicinity as the murderer but it's too late to ask him now.'

The Inspector nodded before moving to top up our glasses. Feeling bold, I asked if he could help.

'Is there any way you would be able to look into his death?' My tone was meek as I anticipated a resounding NO but continued regardless. 'Geraldine tried to get Inspector Borné to look into it, check the details of how he died and she did manage to persuade him to interview everyone to find out where they were and if they knew of any reason why someone would harm him. The problem was that the Inspector doesn't speak any English and he refused to use an interpreter for several members of the family, I'm thinking of Geraldine's oldest children, who are reluctant to speak in French, feeling that their language skills aren't good enough. It meant that their interviews were conducted by using what seemed like charades and in fact someone said the Inspector employed some type of semaphore to get his questions across – preposterous as that sounds.'

The Inspector gazed at me as I babbled, his eyes lighting up in amusement.

'Malarie actually filed an official complaint about him as a detective.' I continued, wincing apologetically and holding my breath for his response.

Raising his eyebrows at that last piece of information he looked away as if genuinely giving my request some consideration. Guessing he would still be reluctant to become involved on someone else's patch, I consoled myself with the fact that at least I'd tried. Finally, he sighed and shook his head.

'If there's no reason to suspect foul play…' He began.

Though expecting this response, I still had to work hard to hide my disappointment.

Since the matter was now closed we sipped our wine in silence for several minutes while watching people sauntering past the café. When the Inspector's phone rang again he scowled, peering at the number for several seconds before excusing himself to answer it. He turned to stare at me while responding and continued to gaze at me as he ended the call.
I met his gaze with a questioning look, curious now as to what the phone call had been about.
'It looks like Malarie was right. Jacques' death is now a murder enquiry.'
'What?' My expression changed to one of shock. Although Malarie had been adamant her father's death was not an accident, it was still hard to accept that he was murdered.
'According to the postmortem, Jacques was dead before he went into the water.'
Stunned, I breathed a heavy sigh. 'So now we have two murders, no motive for either of them and only the family as suspects.'
'We? *Non*, Madame, you need to leave this investigation to the police.'
'But none of the family have any faith in Inspector Borné,' I protested. The Inspector looked uncomfortable. 'And it will be his investigation, not mine.'
'So you want me to leave it to him?' I asked incredulously.
The Inspector glanced at his watch, finished off the wine in his glass and shuffled forward in his seat as if about to stand up.
'Okay,' his voice lowered and he looked uneasy, 'is there an office or study in the house? Could you get in there? Perhaps look through papers, bills etcetera to see if there is anything relevant in there?'
I gazed at him in astonishment. 'What? You want me to sneak in and rake through someone else's things? Break the law in fact?'
He shrugged with a grin. 'It's not like you haven't done it before.'

I flushed, recalling an earlier incident where he'd caught me in a similar position, almost red handed.

'Well, Geraldine took over a downstairs room for a bedroom because she was struggling with the stairs and which I'm guessing used to be another sitting room. There might be paperwork in there so I could try to creep in and have a look I suppose.' I pulled a face feeling rather treacherous, excited and apprehensive all at the same time.

He nodded satisfied then stood up, taking money from his wallet to leave on the table.

At that same moment I spied Marie walking along on the other side of the road and raised a hand to catch her eye when she glanced in our direction. In response she headed toward us.

The Inspector ignored Marie's approach. 'Now I must go Madame but I'll be in touch so we can once again share our information.'

I looked up at him and smiled. 'Okay.'

'*Bonjour*!' Said Marie brightly.

The Inspector now glanced at Marie in surprise as she went to pull a chair across from another table.

'Please, take this Madame. I am leaving.'

She took the offered seat. 'Oh *c'est très gentil, merci.*'

The Inspector turned toward me with a nod. '*À la prochaine.*'

I watched the Inspector walk away while Marie reached across to take a clean glass from a newly laid table nearby and saw him stop to greet a woman who glanced briefly at me and Marie before leaning in to kiss him on both cheeks.

'Didier,' she breathed seductively.

He then escorted the woman away from the café, his hand resting on her lower back.

I raised my eyebrows in a meaningful look at Marie. 'Well, they seem friendly,' I said.

'Not as friendly as you might imagine.' Marie responded with a grin.

'Oh?'

'That's his ex-wife.'

I gave a slow nod, digesting her words and turned again to watch the Inspector and his ex-wife strolling away side by side, his arm now dropped by his side.

'So you were on your way back to the house I presume.'

Marie nodded. 'After my nap I went back to see Hugo as I had left my phone at his place.'

I nodded.

'And Di told me you were summoned again by the Inspector?'

'Actually no. Someone calling themselves the Inspector left a message to meet him, but I don't know who it was. It was purely by chance that I saw the Inspector in here and he claimed not to know anything about it.'

Marie frowned. 'How strange!'

She helped herself to the last of the wine while we both mulled over a reason for the pretence. Unable to conjure up an explanation, I resolved to put it from my mind and told her the news that Jacques' death was now being classed as a murder. As expected she was astonished but like me, was nonplussed about motive and perpetrator. I also told her about how the Inspector had suggested I attempt an illegal search through Geraldine's paperwork to see what I could find. Appalled that I should be considering such a thing she conceded that Geraldine did seem to be confused and perhaps it would help if we could discover if there was an actual will and what was in it. She was also amazed that I'd been given permission by an officer of the law to do it. This led to our reminiscing about our previous foray into that same type of illegal activity and us to giggle uncontrollably.

CHAPTER THIRTEEN

We wandered back to the house while discussing when we might have the opportunity to sneak into Geraldine's room without anyone catching us. Fortunately, it was to happen sooner rather than later. As soon as we returned, Collette appeared and told Marie that Geraldine was keen to speak with her. Marie went straight away, and I returned to our room to find Di writing up information in the form of notes from earlier conversations with members of the family. She said she was aware of Jacques death now being a murder enquiry because Inspector Borné had turned up around ten minutes earlier and had requested all family members accompany him down at the lake and scene of the crime in the hope that it would jog someone's memory with relevant information. I hastily told her about the plan to search Geraldine's room and said that as the house was quiet there was no time like the present. Luckily, Di agreed to take Marie's place without any qualms so we made our way quickly and quietly down the stairs. Keeping my voice low, I explained that Inspector Maupetit had actually sanctioned our activity but would fill her in on the details later. She opened her mouth in a look of astonishment as we went but made no comment. With only a couple of steps left we were forced to a halt when we witnessed Elise leaving Geraldine's room. Instinctively hanging back so she couldn't see us, we watched as she glanced around furtively before quietly closing the door. In a stroke of luck, she chose to go in the opposite direction leading us both to breathe a silent sigh of relief. We then traded meaningful looks before creeping quietly toward the bedroom.

A large double bed took up most of the space and emphasised the personal nature of the room which filled me with a great sense of betrayal.

'What is it exactly that we're looking for?' Whispered Di.

I pulled a face. 'Not sure exactly, a will maybe, if there is one or maybe there's something here that could give us a clue as to the reason for Julien's murder.'

Di nodded and moved quickly toward an antique bureau which sat in the far corner of the room. Pulling down the front to create a writing desk she proceeded to tug at some papers filed messily at one side then peered closely at them.

'Got something?' I whispered loudly as I scanned the bookshelves nearby.

'Not sure, these are from way back.'

She handed me a piece of paper. Regular payments of hundreds of euros to a Victor Blanchet were shown but the date on them was well over thirty years earlier. I shook my head discarding the information as irrelevant. The organization and age of the paperwork seemed to mirror the jumbled state of her book shelves. Di handed me another piece of paper from the same file just as I took a box file down from a shelf.

'Name of the previous owner on this one,' said Di, 'a Madame Vidale.'

'Hmm,' I murmured while I focused on scanning through a stack of household bills in the box file. 'None of it means anything. Is there anything there that resembles a will?'

'No' she replied shaking her head.

A sound from outside made us freeze. Several voices grew louder as they passed the door but then quietened as they moved away toward the other downstairs rooms.

'We should go.' I whispered almost silently.

Di nodded, agreeing.

Leaving everything as we found it, I opened the door slightly and peered out. 'All clear.'

We hurried out and closed the door quietly. My heart was racing.
'Phew!' Di breathed as we climbed the stairs while trying hard to stop from giggling.

We were back several minutes when Marie returned.
'How was Geraldine?' I asked.
'Okay, just a little tired I think.'
I stared at Marie, it was hard to put my finger on what it was but she seemed distant, distracted.
'So did she have something urgent to tell you?'
'*Pas vraiment*, just wanted to find out what we knew, and I did not have much to tell her.'
I nodded, wondering why Geraldine would summon Marie to ask her this when Di and I had spoken to Geraldine earlier that day and already told her the very same thing.
'Well at least you kept her busy while we searched her room, *after* we saw Elise leaving her room.'
Marie's eyebrows rose. 'I wonder what she was up to?' She said somewhat half-heartedly.
I shared a puzzled look with Di.
'Did she say anything about Julien?'
Marie turned pale. '*Non*, nothing.' She went into the bathroom.
'What's going on?' Di mouthed at me.
I shrugged and shook my head, feeling just as nonplussed.
When Marie returned, she appeared a bit more herself. 'Actually Geraldine was rambling a little and said something about not trusting people. She also said something about V.J. again. I couldn't make out what she meant and she started to get a little distressed. Luckily the doctor turned up to take care of her.'
Di looked amazed. 'Again? Two doctor visits in one day.'
Neither of us replied to Di's remark.

'Hm, I wonder who Geraldine can't trust.' I murmured, gazing at Marie who was now focused on folding up some of her clothes.
'So, what did the Inspector want?' Asked Di.
'Well, first of all, he knew nothing...'
My voice trailed off as we saw Marie put on her coat, surprised that she wasn't staying with us while we discussed the information.
'I need some fresh air, so I'll catch up with this later.' She said and without waiting for a response, left the room.
Di and I gazed at each other in surprise.
'She seems troubled. Maybe Geraldine told her about something which upset her.'
I shrugged. 'It certainly seems like it. We'll just have to wait until she's ready to tell us.'

*

The evening meal that evening was a relaxed affair. Collette had put out a buffet of cold meats and salads with instructions to help ourselves. Although the atmosphere was muted, the conversation among the family was polite and once again, I found it hard to contemplate any of them wanting to cause Geraldine harm. On the other hand,
was it so inconceivable that any of them could be faking their geniality? We'd seen Elise acting suspiciously while leaving Geraldine's room so we assumed she wasn't the innocent she made out. Could the others have something to hide? Were they putting up a good show of getting along, perhaps just for us, as outsiders?

CHAPTER FOURTEEN

I received an SMS text the following morning on my phone from the Inspector suggesting we meet for an update. He was obviously eager to discover if I'd found out anything from looking through Geraldine's papers so I agreed to meet him around ten and headed toward the café after breakfast.

The Inspector was hidden behind a newspaper when I arrived, his tiny espresso coffee cup and glass of water already on the table. I sat down opposite and waited, deciding to see how long it would be before he noticed me. The sun was shining in a clear blue sky and there was still an abundance of colour in the hanging baskets and borders surrounding the café as well as roses poking out of the railings in the rose garden opposite so I took the time to simply enjoy the pleasant surroundings and the warmth of the sun. After several minutes I succumbed to impatience and gave up.

'Ahem!'

'Ah, Madame Patterson.' He grinned, folding the paper before placing it on the table. 'I wondered how long you would wait before attracting my attention.'

I threw him an indignant look which only served to amuse him further as he lifted his hand to the waiter. Several minutes later my *grande crème* arrived making me feel, even though it was only my second visit, that I was becoming a regular.

He waited until after my first sip. 'So, any news?'

I relayed any information I could think of since our last update.

'We overhead Julien telling Genevieve that someone had reported him arguing with Jacques about the fishing license.'

The Inspector looking puzzled, repeated slowly. 'Julien told Genevieve that someone…'

Realising at once by his reaction how confusing it all sounded I tried to clarify. 'Suffice is to say that we think Julien told Jacques he couldn't have his fishing license renewed.'

The Inspector nodded slowly, still looking puzzled then disregarding this information changed the subject.

'Were you able to find any relevant paperwork?'
'Well, all we found were some papers which named the previous owner of the house from years ago and some regular payments made to someone. But again this was from a long time ago.'
'Payments?'
'Yes, monthly payments I think.'
'How much?'
'A few hundred, different amounts, but made regularly.'
The Inspector nodded.
'It's not relevant though is it?'
The Inspector raised his eyebrows and shrugged.
'Well, going back to what I said about the fishing license, I was thinking that if Julien had told Jacques he couldn't have the license, maybe they could have argued and Julien could have killed Jacques, maybe even by accident.'
The Inspector nodded. 'Pushed him perhaps? All supposition of course. But then who killed Julien and why?'
We sat in silence with our thoughts for a few minutes then he said.
'Did anyone actually see Julien talking to Jacques?'
'Di said that Elise claimed to have seen Julien…' I stopped mid-sentence when I saw the Inspector narrow his eyes and frown as he tried to keep track once again of the people involved.
'I'll rephrase that, Julien was seen talking to Jacques and it apparently got heated. Jacques was overheard saying that if Henri was alive he'd issue the license without a problem. Julien reportedly said 'well he's not so his mother can do what she likes as it's her land.' Then Jacques responded by saying something like 'we'll see about that.' but…' I paused again.
'But?'

'Well Elise and Julien argued at dinner recently and quite vehemently so I wouldn't be surprised if Elise was just trying to put Julien in the frame for Jacques' murder. I could be wrong, but you know, maybe?'
The Inspector looked thoughtful but made no comment.
'Also I spied Elise coming out of Geraldine's bedroom when I knew Geraldine wasn't in there. So what was she doing in there?'
The Inspector didn't respond so I changed the subject.
'Collette said that Malarie was working for Geraldine against her father's wishes.'
'And you think that is relevant?' Another puzzled look from the Inspector.
'Well, Jacques apparently forbade Malarie to work for Geraldine and was angry when he found out.'
'For what reason? Because of the fishing license?'
I shook my head. 'By all accounts he told her it wasn't safe.'
The Inspector frowned. 'How so?'
I shrugged.
'So Jacques believed it wasn't safe to work for Geraldine, but we don't know why.' He muttered, seeming bemused.
I gasped. 'Could that have been why he was killed?'
'It sounds more plausible than arguing over a fishing license, though I have known of people murdered for less,' remarked the Inspector drily.

I left the Inspector to stroll back to the house while reflecting on our conversation. From his response to my information about Jacques, I got the impression that he didn't seem keen to pursue the idea Jacques had been murdered. Could it simply be that he didn't want to step on Inspector Borné's toes or did he genuinely believe there were no suspicious circumstances. Because of his lack of interest I'd been reluctant to mention how Geraldine was given to rambling about

someone known as V.J. or that she kept saying she couldn't trust someone. Was I wrong not to have told him?
I shook my head as if to clear it. Potentially two murders had been committed and yet motives still escaped us. I breathed a heavy sigh. Maybe it was just as well that I only had a few more days before returning home since we still hadn't found any information to help Geraldine, maybe because my thoughts were increasingly consumed with my impending lifestyle change. By the time I reached the house I was feeling rather despondent.

*

Sophie called on WhatsApp to ask how things were going. Di I sat on the bed and peered into the tiny phone screen while Marie lounged on her bed opposite scrolling through her own phone. We tried to recall everything we knew to bring her up to date.
'Why couldn't Malarie work at the house. What objections could her father have?' She asked.
We both shrugged.
'Guess we'll never find out now. We're wondering if there's something he knew about that we don't.'
I glanced across at Marie to note her reaction, seeing as she'd been a bit subdued since her last meeting with Geraldine which we felt was because she keeping something from us. I knew she'd be listening even though she made a show of being engrossed in her phone.
Di told Sophie about searching for paperwork in Geraldine's room.
'It's a huge room.' Remarked Di.
'Looks like a big house,' nodded Sophie 'It's a wonder how she could afford to buy it if she was on her own with two children and her only income at the time was probably child support from her ex-husband.'
We nodded in agreement.
'She used to do some freelance ghost writing.' Interrupted Marie.

'Oh,' I replied. 'Did you hear that Sophie? Geraldine used to earn money as a freelance ghost writer.'

She raised her eyebrows. 'It must have paid well.' She said sceptically.

I nodded. 'The problem is that because of her illness or maybe the drugs she's taking, she seems to spend a lot of time rambling on about things which don't make any sense.'

'Like what?'

'Well, Marie said she keeps mentioning someone called Veejay. Though we don't know if that's the initials V.J. Anyway, the only papers we found in her room were from a long time ago so we've decided they weren't relevant and we're thinking trying to get another look.'

'So what were the papers you found? The old ones?'

'Oh, something about a house sale and payments made to a Victor Blanchet. The previous owner's name was on some of them too, Emily Vidale'. I glanced at Di for her to corroborate. She nodded.

'Did you say Victor Blanchet?' Interrupted Marie with a stunned expression.

I nodded. 'D'you know the name?'

'Is there something else?' Asked Sophie, clearly wondering why we weren't looking at her through the screen anymore as we were both now giving our attention to Marie.

'Hello?' She called. Once again we ignored Sophie while waiting for Marie to enlighten us but she simply gazed at us as if in shock.

I glanced back at Sophie, reminded she was still there. 'Can we call you back Sophie? Something's come up.'

'Of course. Speak soon.' She ended the call.

'So? Do you know the name?' I repeated.

Marie took a deep breath. 'That was my father's name.'

'Really?' said Di wide eyed.

Marie sighed and looked awkward. 'I might as well tell you. Geraldine told me in our last conversation that she had an affair with my father.'
'Oh!' Gasped Di.
'She claims she didn't know he was married and when she found out she called it off.'
'And this was when?'
'Before she met Henri.' Said Marie looking uncomfortable.
'Oh, so that's why your mother left him maybe.' Said Di gently.
Marie shrugged.
I frowned. 'I'm wondering why Geraldine made him regular payments of hundreds of euros?'
Marie shrugged again.
'Hmm, I can see why you would be shocked about hearing that but unfortunately, it doesn't seem to have anything to do with Jacques or Julien's death.' The remark sounded insensitive and I regretted it instantly.
'Does anyone else feel like we're getting nowhere?' Asked Di.
'Maybe we should take some time out?' I suggested trying to placate Marie. 'Why don't we do a bit of sightseeing tomorrow.'
Di agreed eagerly but although Marie agreed, her weak smile gave away her sullen thoughts.

CHAPTER FIFTEEN

It was another mild sunny autumn morning when we set off for *Nanteuil En Valée*, a village east of Ruffec. Arriving after only a short fifteen minute drive, Di parked the car near the *Abbaye* Notre Dame which we were fortunate to find was open that day for visitors. After taking some time to wander around the ruins and visit the small museum with its excavation displays, we strolled up into the village.

Halting to decide on our next port of call next to the *Fontaine St Jean*, a small stone fountain in the centre of the village, we found ourselves admiring a nearby *auberge* with its part timbered façade. As we'd forgone breakfast to make an early start, the idea of starting lunch at midday was appealing so we went toward it just as two waiters were making finishing touches to the tables for diners. As the sun felt warm and there was very little breeze we opted to take up a table outside in front of a large grid type window and bordering the road.

Being the first customers, the waiter was quick to bring bread and a carafe of water while we scanned our menus, and was then just as quick to take our orders. I chose Salmon *Chiffonade* for an *entrée* with Marie and Di choosing the Boar *Terrine*. The food was delicious and we engaged in lighthearted chatter which continued into our main course of beef *bourguignonne*.

Amazingly no one had yet brought up the subject of the murders. Then, out of the blue, while deliberating whether to opt for dessert or cheese to end our meal, Di said, 'To address the elephant in the room,' she paused, her gaze resting on me, causing Marie to look puzzled.

'I'm assuming you'll be selling the house Catherine?'

Taken aback at her candour I was struck silent for a moment while I considered how to answer.

'I suppose.'

Marie stared at me in amazement. 'And you don't want to stay, even without Karl?'

I raised my eyebrows in surprise while Di gave Marie a bemused look. 'Why would I do that?'

She shrugged. 'Some people have long distance relationships and are happy that way, besides what are you going back to? Shouldn't you also think about what you want and not just Karl?'

I shook my head, nonplussed at her suggestion. 'We're happily married and we came here together on the understanding that should

one of us not be completely happy then we would return to the UK. I've known Karl has been less than content for a while so this opportunity he's been given is going to be good for him.'
'But not for you,' insisted Marie.
'Well, I,' I stuttered, feeling ambushed yet conceding that she'd struck a nerve. Fortunately Di came to my rescue.
'Well, it's early days isn't it? Didn't you say Karl hasn't given them a definitive answer to their offer? So, I'm guessing you'll both be giving it some serious thought.'
'Of course.'
'So, no use in worrying about it yet.' Di smiled cheerily.
I nodded with a weak smile and Marie shrugged but let the matter drop.
Waiting for our dessert after opting to finish our meal with *crème caramel* and coffee, our conversation turned to the murders. We discussed how the police seemed to be no further forward in finding Julien's murderer nor with discovering any definitive motive. We also reiterated how Geraldine's children seemed to be amiable and no one seemed looking to do her any harm. Finally we decided it was frustrating going over the same facts and information and coming up with nothing.
After we left the restaurant we decided to visit an arboretum garden on the banks of the river Argentor nearby, deciding it would be an excellent way to walk off our meal. The sloping ground which overlooked the Argentor diversion canal was bordered with low planting boxwood. Dwarf lonicera lined the paths. Strolling past various large trees such as magnolia, araucaria, sapo pine, cedar we went to stand next to a large pond, admiring the aquatic plants in and around the pond where I named those I recognized next to the well-known water lilies, such as water buttercups, pondweed, arum rushes and reeds. A jet of water appeared intermittently from the centre which

was a delight. But overall the garden felt very calming and helped me to push thoughts of murderers and moving home far from my mind.

CHAPTER SIXTEEN

Malarie informed us that neither she nor Collette would be around to prepare dinner. Some of the family had already made dinner reservations and I heard that David and Elise had gone out for the day and had not yet returned. Marie decided to speak with Geraldine in case she'd been informed of any progress in the investigation so I went to fetch two cups of tea from the kitchen for me and Di. I was on the way back to our room, concentrating on not spilling the tea when I came to a halt outside Geraldine's room, having nearly walked into Celia. I grinned apologetically but glimpsed a flash of panic in her eyes. Looking down at the cups in my hand, her expression changed to one of concern.

'She's resting.' She whispered.

'Yes of course,' I nodded, realising that she'd been trying close the door as quietly as possible.

*

Wearing only light jackets we sat on the terrace of a bar opposite the café where I'd met the Inspector the day before. Instead of admiring the floral displays, the fading light allowed us to appreciate the colourful twinkling fairy lights which festooned the awnings of the bar and nearby restaurant.

We'd just ordered our aperitifs when Marie sat forward preparing to discuss her meeting earlier with Geraldine.

'Was Celia in the room with you and Geraldine by the way?' I interrupted as she was about to begin.

Marie looked puzzled and shook her head. 'I spoke to Geraldine in her conservatory. I didn't see Celia at all.'
'Oh,' I frowned.
'What is it?' Asked Di.
'So, Marie was talking to Geraldine in the conservatory while I made us cups of tea. Then when I was returning to our room Celia was coming out of Geraldine's room and made out that Geraldine was in there by telling me she was resting.'
Marie and Di looked at each other in confusion.
'So Celia was in Geraldine's room without Geraldine.'
'And Elise has been in Geraldine's room without Geraldine.'
'As have we.' Said Di with a guilty look.
'Everyone is clearly looking for something.' Observed Marie.
We traded thoughtful glances as we considered their intentions.
'Anyway,' said Marie 'back to the content of our conversation. Geraldine has told me that Victor Blanchet, my *father*, was in fact a *notaire* and involved in the sale of her house *but* she point blank refused to discuss anything further.'
'Hm.' I murmured.
'She also mentioned V.J. again.'
'Oh?' Di and I said in unison.
She nodded. 'She said, and I quote, 'that damn V.J.' then said something about being 'nothing but trouble.''
'Why did she mention him or *her*?' asked Di.
Marie shook her head. 'Just came out with it when I asked about whether Victor Blanchet was a *notaire*.'
'You know it seems to me that we have two mysteries here and maybe it's just me but I can't see anyway they're related.' I said after a brief consideration of the situation. 'On the one hand there's the death of Jacques and Julien and on the other is a mystery we've discovered about Geraldine's background.'

Di nodded in agreement. 'Yeah nothing seems to go together and actually we don't even know if Jacques and Julien's murders are connected to each other either so there could even be three mysteries!' I stared at Marie thoughtfully, wondering if she would prefer to know more about her father now that he was intricated in Geraldine's affairs. 'Perhaps, since we can't get anywhere with Jacques and Julien's murders we should leave them to the police and just spend the last few days we have here unravelling Geraldine's past.'

Di glanced at Marie to check her reaction and was surprised to see Marie reluctantly agree.

As if a weight had been lifted, the conversation from then on was more light hearted. Marie's manner became more cheery, much like her usual self, as she gradually acknowledged her own curiosity about her father. She even suggested a group trip when it was all over to make up for this one being so gloomy. Then with a sad look she added, 'if you are still living in France of course.'

Distracted, I didn't respond. My thoughts were now going over the last few days of our visit. I decided there didn't seem much point to meeting up with Inspector Maupetit for any more updates because of our decision to stop investigating the murders. A conclusion which suddenly overwhelmed me with disappointment, before I began persuading myself that it might be better to meet him one last time so I could tell him in person. At least then I could discover, just out of interest, if he had unearthed any new information about the murders.

'So are you going to make notes as we go through this as a separate issue now?' Di was saying, giving me an odd look.

I gazed at her with a blank expression before quickly coming to my senses. 'Oh yes', I said, fumbling as I took out my notebook and brought my mind to present company.

'So, regular payments made to Victor Blanchet went on for several months then stopped.' I began. 'Payments made *after* the sale of the house so if he was the *notaire* that dealt with the house sale, and we are now fairly sure that he was, why would they continue?'

'Payments for his services as a *notaire*? Maybe Geraldine had to pay in installments.' Suggested Marie.

I nodded in agreement 'If she couldn't afford to pay in one go I suppose, though I find it hard to believe that the total amount, which amounted to over a thousand euros, was just for someone doing the legal work on a house sale. Doesn't it seem excessive?'

'I suppose if the house is expensive, there is a higher legal bill.' Mused Marie thoughtfully.

'What about blackmail?' Suggested Di in a low voice, her eyes darting left and right in case of eavesdroppers. Although echoing my passing thought, which I hadn't voiced for fear of offending Marie, I attempted a shocked look at Di's suggestion.

Surprisingly, Marie took the comment in her stride.

'If it was blackmail what would be the reason?' Marie asked innocently.

We fell silent.

'What if…' said Di gazing at Marie. 'You said your mother and Geraldine were friends.'

Marie nodded.

'What if Victor wanted money from Geraldine to stop him from telling your mother that she'd had an affair with him.'

'But wouldn't that give him up as an adulterer as well? He wouldn't just ruin their friendship but also his marriage.' I countered.

Marie snorted. 'I don't think my mother would have been surprised by his infidelity. She never said anything specific about him but one of the things I worked out was that he played around.'

I couldn't help but gaze at Marie in wonder. She had repeated the pattern by also marrying a man who had reputedly 'played around' as she called it, however she had also confessed to having had one or two liaisons herself.

'On the other hand, I do know she valued her friendship with Geraldine so perhaps knowing about the affair would have drove a wedge between them. So maybe you're right and it was blackmail.' Marie conceded.

I lifted my pen to make a note of our conclusions. 'So we're saying the blackmail was probably because of the infidelity?' I waited for the others to respond.

Di nodded and Marie shrugged. 'Maybe', 'Could be' they replied.

'So now what about this Veejay,' I said looking down at my notes. 'I'll write it down as initials and we'll assume it was another person for now.'

They nodded in agreement.

'Could it be another *notaire*?' Asked Di.

'Perhaps the one who drew up her will,' suggested Marie with a little more enthusiasm, getting into the spirit of things.

'If there even is a will' I pulled a face before making a note about needing to find out more about the will.

'Well, everyone seems to be looking for one.' Remarked Di. Marie and I nodded, silently agreeing that's probably what Elise and Celia had been looking for.

'We still don't know what the note was about, you know the one that invited Marie to the boat house.' Said Di.

We gazed at each other vacantly. 'Any ideas?' I said, giving Marie a direct look, in the hope that she might have more of a notion as to why she'd been contacted.

She sighed. 'I have been thinking about this and I know we're all guessing that it was Julien who wrote it.'

Di and me nodded since we'd decided that was the most likely.

'I've thought about what Julien would want to tell me and the only thing I keep coming up with is that he has just been told Henri was not his father and Geraldine has told me she had an affair with my father so with another guess…'

'Oh, of course.' I gasped, glancing at Di to see if she'd grasped what Marie was saying.

'So that would have made Julien your half-brother.' Di became wide eyed, evidence of the penny dropping.

Marie nodded. 'It is a guess of course but I could try to ask Geraldine, see if she will confirm it.'

I sighed. 'So, are we now assuming that Geraldine told Julien his father's name? And that name was Victor Blanchet?'

'So are we are saying he knew his name?' asked Di.

'Well, If Julien knew his father's name, he could have researched who Victor was, found out who he was married to and that would have led him to Marie being Victor's daughter. So I suppose it could be the reason he wanted to speak to you.' Di gazed at Marie.

'Meaning Julien wanted to tell Marie that he knew who his father was and wanted to find out whether Marie knew about him *and* what she knew about him?' I gazed at Di doubtfully. 'And if not, let her know he was her half-brother?'

Marie shook her head in bemusement. 'But why the secret *rendez vous*?'

'Yeah, and strange that he needed to meet at midnight to discuss it,' said Di drily.

I sighed again in frustration. 'So much guesswork, we really need to get some solid facts.'

They nodded in agreement.

At least we now had a plan to focus specifically on Geraldine's background so I put away my notebook. We finished our Kiki

Vendéen aperitifs and ordered a bottle of wine along with *croques monsieurs*, since it had been several hours since our lunch.

Several glasses of wine later and we began to reminisce about the murders and investigations we'd been involved in during the last few years and laughed about how we'd irritated the Inspector with our interference. Finally expressing satisfaction about how we'd finally coaxed him into accepting our help in his investigations.

During a lull in our conversation we became conscious of the buzz of conversation and laughter around us. Throwing a cursory glance around the café I noticed that most of the tables were now taken and stared as a man and a familiar looking woman were about to sit down near the entrance. I shot Marie a quizzical look to which she nodded, confirming my unvoiced suspicion that the woman was the Inspector's ex-wife. Di turned to peer curiously.

'She's quite a striking looking woman,' I remarked.

Di and Marie agreed.

'Well the Inspector's an attractive man so they must have made quite a couple.' Remarked Di.

Marie looked pointedly at me. 'Yes the Inspector is rather handsome in a rugged sort of way don't you think Cat'rine?'

I shrugged noncommittedly. 'I suppose.'

*

Before we went to bed that night I emailed Sophie as I wanted to bring her up to date and tell her we'd decided not to investigate Julien and Jacques death but simply concentrate on looking into Geraldine's background to help Marie find out about her father. I commented that it seemed a strange thing to be doing since Marie hadn't been interested in finding out anything about him when we first arrived. I told her that I thought that discovering his name in Geraldine's papers as the *notaire* and Julien as her half-brother made her curious so she now wanted to solve the mystery of why Geraldine had paid him so much money. We'd judged that the amount she'd paid seemed high just to pay for his services as a *notaire* so we were going to try to question Geraldine, despite her reluctance and confusion, to find out more. I also told her that we believed someone called V.J. was also involved in her past and we'd decided it may have been another *notaire*, perhaps one involved in making a will, if there actually was one. I told her how Celia and Elise had been spotted leaving Geraldine's room and we suspected they were looking for a will. I signed off by saying that if Geraldine had been more cleared headed and open to our questions we wouldn't have a mystery to solve. I also said despite declaring no further interest in Julien's murder I couldn't help but think that knowing the contents and beneficiaries of a will might give us some clue as to a motive for his murder.

CHAPTER SEVENTEEN

We had just returned to our room after breakfast when I received an SMS text from the Inspector. He asked if I could meet him at a restaurant in town for lunch for our update. I gazed at the screen, considering the change of venue from sharing a table for coffee to an actual meal. It seemed more of a commitment. Unsure whether to meet him or not, I mean, was there really any point if we weren't involved in the investigation? What would we talk about? I hesitated over the response. Di noticed my hesitation and asked if everything was ok. I sighed, deciding to be candid. 'I was supposed to be meeting the Inspector for an update but actually we've got nothing else that I can tell him now so I'm wondering if there's anything we would talk about.'

'And?' asks Di guessing there was more and waiting for me to elaborate.

'And,' I paused, struggling with whether to tell her. 'He wants me to meet him at *La Fleur*, which is a restaurant so we're clearly going to have lunch.'
'And you don't want to have lunch?' She asked innocently.
I felt awkward. 'Should I be having lunch with him when there isn't anything to discuss about the investigation?'
Di shrugged, a puzzled look on her face. 'Then you could just enjoy the lunch, which is all it is.' She paused, an odd look on her face. 'Isn't it?'
'Yes of course.' I laughed lightly.
Picking up my phone I stared at the text again but sensing Di's eyes on me I threw it onto the bed. 'I'll reply later.' I shrugged with a forced casual tone.

I decided not to meet the Inspector and replied simply that I couldn't make it. Almost at once I felt torn. This would be the last time I would be involved in any investigation with him. Surely I should let him know, I owed him that much. Regretting my decision I resolved to kill two birds with one stone. I needed to go into town to use the cash machine anyway, so if I timed it just right, I would be able to catch the Inspector on his way to or actually in the restaurant. I would explain that I'd been able to make it after all but couldn't stay for lunch as I was there to let him know that we hadn't discovered anything useful and would let the police get on with the investigation without us. And, if I was truthful to myself, so that we could speak for one last time as my way of saying goodbye.
Wandering into the restaurant, I glanced around, suddenly unsure as to whether the Inspector would even be there. Maybe he would have gone to the restaurant only if I'd agreed to meet him? A waiter approached to ask if I had a reservation. I shook my head, once again having second thoughts about whether I should be there. Then, just as I

was frantically conjuring up an excuse to leave, I caught sight of the Inspector at a table next to the window, gazing at a menu with a bottle of wine already on the table while chatting on his phone. He looked relaxed and even chuckled at something he heard. I hesitated. It was clear he hadn't noticed me and was obviously still going to have lunch whether he was with anyone else or not.
'Madame?' The waiter was hovering expectantly.
On the spur of the moment I decided that since it would likely be our last meeting I might as well just arrive unannounced and declare that I could make it for lunch after all.
'I'm er meeting someone,' I said and gestured toward the Inspector before heading toward his table.
The Inspector ended his call just as he noticed me and reacted with a look of surprise.
'Managed to make it after all,' I said breathlessly as if I'd arrived in a hurry. I pulled out the chair opposite.
The Inspector's expression changed at once to one of discomfort as his focus flicked to someone approaching from behind me. Following his gaze, I swung round to find myself looking into the eyes of the woman I now knew to be his ex-wife.
Her cold stare moved from me to the Inspector. 'Didier?' She purred.
'Natalie, er this is…' He began.
Instantly realizing he was there to have lunch with his ex-wife and not alone, I cringed inwardly. Forcing a light laugh, I interrupted him.
'Just on my way.'
Her eyes flicked over me with a look I could only describe as contempt before she took possession of the chair and went to sit down. Meanwhile the Inspector had stood up. 'Madame Patterson…' He started with a concerned look.
His ex-wife was now perusing the menu and making a great show of ignoring me. Feigning confidence yet feeling numb with

embarrassment I forced a casual tone. 'I'll catch you later with any relevant information but I'll leave you now to your lunch. Goodbye.' I turned and left, assuming as I reached the door that I was already forgotten.

*

I walked back to the house briskly while berating myself for going to the restaurant. How embarrassing Catherine! If you tell someone you can't make it then there's no point turning up later expecting that person to be waiting for you. But couldn't he have told me he was waiting for his ex-wife the instant he saw me? Did he really get a chance? Didn't she turn up only seconds after I did? And what a look she gave me! I breathed a heavy sigh. Just have to play it cool when I next see him. Make sure he knows I thought nothing of it. Of course, I made no mention of the incident to Di and Marie. Just thinking about it made me cringe.

*

Marie had gone downstairs to check what time we were expected for dinner and returned several minutes later looking animated. 'Guess who I saw leaving Geraldine's room.' She asked rhetorically and without giving us a chance to reply. 'While Geraldine was chatting to Irène in the dining room.'
Di and I exchanged blank looks.
'Anne!'
We both raised our eyebrows in surprise.
'When I caught sight of her she was looking around as she closed the door. She looked very suspicious so I stayed out of the way and she didn't see me watching her.'
We gazed around at each other, eyes wide.
'Another one!' Gasped Di.
Marie nodded. 'All looking for a will?'

I nodded slowly. 'What else could it be?'
Di narrowed her eyes. 'Hm, in cahoots or acting alone d'you think?'

*

We entered the dining room while the family were having a conversation about their plans to return home. I wondered, while listening, if the police would allow the family to leave while there was still a murder investigation ongoing. From their discussion it seemed none of the family members regarded it as pertinent.

Elise announced that as they'd been invited under false pretences, namely for the reading of a will which she claimed didn't exist, they should be free to leave at any time. Her confidence about the lack of a will made me think we'd been right in assuming she'd been in Geraldine's room searching for one. Clearly she hadn't found it.

David agreed with his sister that there was no reason to stay any longer and stated he was planning to leave in a couple of days. This show of solidarity meant I couldn't help but speculate further. As he and Elise were close, I thought it was highly likely she'd told him about the search or had even instigated it.

Celia muttered that it couldn't be helped if Geraldine was so unwell that the reading of a will, if there was one, had been ignored or even forgotten about. Knowing she had also been seen acting furtively on her way out of Geraldine's room, we'd surmised after also looking for the will, I studied her expression. Was her comment meant to hide the fact that she couldn't find a will either?

Meanwhile Billy had muttered in agreement which made me stare at him in turn. Did he know about Celia searching Geraldine's room?

I glanced at Anne to check her reaction, knowing she'd been another one found leaving Geraldine's room while acting surreptitiously, but her face gave nothing away. She was undoubtedly listening to the chatter but chose to remain tight lipped. Irène, on the other hand, was looking decidedly uncomfortable which I thought interesting. Did she know anything about the will, if in fact there was one?

'Just out of interest how was mum diagnosed?' Asked Anne changing the subject. 'She hasn't been keen to talk about it apart from telling us she's getting treatment. I mean was it just a routine check?'

'She was having headaches.' Replied Irène.

'Collette mentioned Collette had been hallucinating at times and she was sent for tests to the local clinic by her GP.' Added Billy.

Irène looked at Anne. 'And then the doctor arrived to administer medication as well as performing regular checkups.'

'It sounds like she's getting the best care.' Mused Celia as she went to move dishes so Collette could place the food on the table.

'And she told inoperable relatively quickly?' Asked Anne, her tone serious.

Irène nodded sadly. 'It's mainly just pain relief she receives but the doctor's so good with her, he's here a lot.'

'I think he was part of the SAMU team when father had his heart attack after they called it in as an emergency.' Nodded Elise.

Everyone quietly digested the information just as Billy got up to fill everyone's wine glass.

A short while later Collette entered the room followed by Malarie with more dishes.

Surprised to see Malarie so soon after her father's death, everyone expressed their condolences. She thanked them but kept her eyes downcast as if unwilling to allow their kindness to penetrate a defensive wall she'd no doubt built to protect herself.

Geraldine didn't make an appearance at all during dinner.

CHAPTER EIGHTEEN

Geraldine arrived while we were having breakfast the following morning to thank us for our help. Disappointed that we were leaving before discovering any information about her dead cat and who in the family was plotting her demise, she said she was nevertheless grateful that Marie had opted to stay a little longer in the hope of a breakthrough. Still wondering if she'd made up the story about the cat and having found no one in the family who appeared in any way a threat we humoured her, smiling and agreeing it was a shame that we had to leave so soon.

Di and I were putting our bags in her car when Inspector Maupetit arrived. Having hoped to avoid meeting him before we left, I pretended not to see him as he headed in our direction. Unfortunately, I was too slow to escape into the car.

'You are leaving today?' He asked as I pushed down the lid of the boot and Di climbed in the driving seat.

'Yes,' I replied frostily walking past him to the passenger side of the car. Sensing him waiting expectantly I half turned toward him while taking hold of the door handle.

'I'm here to take over from Inspector Borné,' he explained.

'That's nice,' I replied, acting deliberately obtuse.

He frowned and was about to move away when he thought twice about it, hesitating. 'The misunderstanding yesterday…' he began in a conciliatory tone.

I feigned a lighthearted laugh as I opened the car door. 'Don't worry about it. I still managed to get lunch.'

Feeling his gaze on me as I climbed into the car, I turned, regarding him steadily.

'I assume we don't need to stay to be questioned again,' My tone was defiant.

He raised an eyebrow. 'I know where you live.' He said drily.
I nodded then slammed the door shut.
Di gave me a concerned look. 'Problem?'
I forced a smile. 'No, no problem.'
I deliberately looked in the opposite direction from where the Inspector was standing as Di pulled the car out of the drive.

*

Feeling glad to be home, I made a short trip to the supermarket before settling in to check my emails. There were several requests for information about the gîte and queries about when rooms would be available in the *chambres d'hotes* which I was reluctant to answer. If Karl and I were serious about selling then it was pointless taking reservations. I decided therefore that the best use of my time would be to tidy up the garden, focusing on pruning back several shrubs. Then I could check the rooms in the *chambres d'hotes* and gîte for any cosmetic improvements.

Later in the day I called both Chloe and Aiden on WhatsApp and explained that it was likely we'd be selling up and moving back to the UK. Despite them expressing delight at being able to visit more often they also voiced disappointment at the decision, acknowledging that we'd developed a thriving business in France as well as how much we both seemed to enjoy the lifestyle. When the call ended I sat for several minutes mulling over the inevitable disruption to our lives from returning to the UK.

CHAPTER NINETEEN

I picked up a pair of secateurs from the potting shed with the intention of wandering the garden in search of pruning tasks when I involuntarily found myself staring at seedlings in a tray. My thoughts grew dark with the realization that there was no point in propagating any more plants for our garden. Overwhelmed suddenly with sadness, I blinked back tears and pulled a tissue from my pocket while trudging back to the house.

I had only taken a few steps when I came face to face with Sergeant Laurent.

Seeing my distress he immediately pulled out a clean, pressed white handkerchief and offered it to me. I shook my head, hurriedly drying my eyes with a tissue.

'Thank you, I'm fine,' I attempted a smile, blinking rapidly.

The sergeant accepted my response with an awkward look. Finally he opened his mouth to speak but didn't get a chance.

Lesley was marching across the garden. 'Catherine! Oh and it's Théo isn't it? Sergeant Laurent?'

Théo returned Lesley's bright smile, looking somewhat relieved. Taking in my tear stained face she said kindly.

'I came to invite you for coffee Catherine.' Then ensuring I couldn't refuse she added. 'I have cake!'

I couldn't help but respond with a grin. Pleased with my response, Lesley turned to Théo.

'And you too Sergeant Laurent. Whynot join us for coffee?'

'Well…' he hesitated.

'Oh don't worry, there's no alcohol involved.' She chuckled. 'It will give us a chance to apologise.'

Théo grinned, 'Okay.'

Lesley led us across to the side of her house. A round wrought iron table sat under her newly built pergola surrounded by blooming dahlias and brightly coloured cosmos.

She turned to us in delight as she offered us our seats.

'I feel like this will christen our new pergola,' she said excitedly.

I forced a cheery smile. 'It looks great!'

We sat down just as Tim, her husband, arrived with a tray laden with coffee pot and cups. After only a brief greeting he disappeared into the house again only to return within minutes holding a plate on which sat a large gateau.

'Coffee and walnut,' he announced as he placed it on the table.

I saw Théo's eyes light up.

'So how come we're graced with your company?' Asked Tim as he cut into the cake, placing portions carefully onto serving plates.

Théo accepted his graciously. 'The Inspector is in Nantes and wouldn't be able to stop by on his way to Ruffec until the end of the week so he asked me to check in case there'd been any developments that we didn't know about.'

'Ah so the investigation in Ruffec is still…' began Tim.

'…ongoing.' Nodded Théo as took up his dessert fork.

We all spent a few minutes enjoying the cake and coffee.

'So are you back in this area to work or are you also returning to Ruffec?' I asked Théo.

'I'm back here as there aren't as many of us needed in Ruffec now. I also live close by so it was easy to drop in here on my way home.'

'Are you married Théo?' Asked Lesley, openly prying.

Théo beamed and immediately pulled out a photograph from his wallet.

'*Oui*, and I have a two-year-old son.' He announced proudly, handing over the photograph for us to crow over.

'Did you get into a lot of trouble with the Inspector?' I asked, handing his photograph back.

He grinned and shrugged before finishing his coffee. 'Just a little.' He went to stand up while gazing at Tim and Lesley. '*Merci bien* for the delicious cake and coffee but I must be on my way.'

Tim and Lesley were all smiles. 'You're most welcome,' replied Tim kindly.

Théo glanced across the table at me. 'So nothing new to report to the Inspector.'

I was about to shake my head when I thought better of it. 'Actually, you can tell him that he won't be hearing from us, or me anymore as we've decided that since we're struggling to find any clues we can't help the police any further.'

He raised his eyebrows in surprise. 'Okay.'

Lesley chuckled. 'I bet the Inspector will be glad to hear about that!'

Once Théo had left, Lesley turned to me while Tim busied himself with clearing away the plates while offering to bring out more coffee.

'Might as well enjoy the outdoors while we can since it's supposed to turn cooler and wetter from next week.' He said to no one in particular.

'So Catherine did I hear you correctly?' Lesley gazed at me in surprise. 'You're not involving yourself anymore in those murders?'

I sighed. 'We had to decide because we were getting nowhere. So, because Marie became interested in finding out about her father we decided to focus on him instead.'

Lesley nodded. 'I see. And that's because you're guessing that he was blackmailing Geraldine. But what about Geraldine, how does this help her?'

'Well, I doubt it does but as it's something to do with her past and as she seems to be fretting about something *in* her past, maybe we'll be able to provide some sort of resolution for her. Of course, Marie is staying in Ruffec a while longer to search local archives for her father's death certificate. See if she can find a cause of death.'

'If, as you say Inspector Borné has been working in Ruffec for a long time, maybe he can remember her father. But then I suppose that's only if Marie finds out he died in suspicious circumstances. It's a long shot I think.'

Tim returned with a fresh pot of coffee and the conversation turned to Karl's new job. I reminded them that he hadn't actually agreed to take it yet but it was likely. A short while later a car pulled up next to the house. Stickers on the side showed the car as belonging to the *immobilier* . Lesley reluctantly accepted I needed to leave to show the agent around the property.

I ignored a phone call while the *immobilier* was at the house so checked for the caller once she'd gone. Marie had left a message. She said Inspector Maupetit had agreed to ask if Inspector Borné could remember her father. She said she felt optimistic about it, saying that as he was a *notaire* and therefore a fairly prominent member of a small community, Borné might recall how he died. She said that she hadn't disclosed to Maupetit that they'd come across Victor Blanchet's name amongst Geraldine's papers but had pretended that she was just curious to find out what happened to her father. She said Maupetit had been happy to agree to her request. She finished by saying she would be in touch as soon as she managed to find out anything else from Geraldine.

*

Sure enough, only a short while later while I was wasting time on Rightmove looking at property in the UK, I received a WhatsApp call from Marie. She said Inspector Maupetit had been in touch and it turned out that Inspector Borné could remember Victor Blanchet. I expressed amazement at both the rapid response from the Inspector as well as the fact that Inspector Borné could recall the details from such a long time ago.

Marie's face was serious 'That is because Victor Blanchet was found at the bottom of some steps in a park near his home. The same park bordering Geraldine's land. It was reported that he had been drinking and his death ruled as a tragic accident.'

'It was definitely an accident? No questions raised about it?'
Marie shook her head. 'Not recorded as suspicious at all.'
'Hm, so maybe it was an accident,' I replied. 'Though I think it begs the question: did Inspector Borné investigate thoroughly?'
'*Exactement,*' replied Marie having the same thought.
I changed the subject. 'Has the Inspector disclosed any further information about Jacques or Julien's deaths?'
'*Non*, but no one in the family seems to know anything so I don't think there can by any new leads. Anyway, after being given permission to leave, David and Elise left yesterday. Irène is staying a few more days but Billy, Celia and Anne are leaving tomorrow.'
I nodded, 'It seems to me like the police have given up.'
'I agree.'
Finally, after expressing bemusement that the police were no nearer to catching the murderers than when the crimes were first committed, we agreed to stay in touch.

CHAPTER TWENTY

I was enjoying a cup of coffee the next morning when I received an email from Sophie. She was replying to the email I sent during my stay in Ruffec. She wrote that she agreed with our decision about the best course of action being to focus on one mystery at a time and allow the police to investigate the murders. She also went along with our views on family members leaving Geraldine's room while glancing around furtively, definitely seemed to be suspicious and agreed with our consensus that they were likely to be searching for the 'elusive' will. Sophie then offered to help with discovering who V.J. might be. She said our notion that it could be another *notaire* was valid and again agreed that it might therefore be someone who had a legal role in the writing of a will. Finally, she proposed that she should try to discover if there was still, or had been, a *notaire* with those initials in the Ruffec area.

Sophie's previous experience as an investigative journalist usually meant she came up trumps with information we lacked and had been an invaluable resource in our search for knowledge related to previous murders we'd helped investigate. I was therefore pleased to read her positive response but of course, I'd come to expect nothing less. The feeling I got from her email was that she was optimistic about her chances and I couldn't help but smile at the thought.

*

'*Bonjour*!'

I turned to find Sophie at the door of the *gîte* while I was inspecting the kitchen cupboards for any problems.

I smiled in response. 'Ah hello!'

'Thought I might as well pop in rather than correspond by email again.

I nodded, 'Great! Coffee?'

'Lovely,' she beamed.

A short while later we sat at the kitchen table.

'Okay, so I'm struggling to find a *notaire* with initials V.J.'

'Oh,' I said, unable to hide my disappointment.

'Is there anyone else it could be? I mean, when Geraldine mentions this person does she talk about anything else at the same time.'

I thought for a moment. 'Well, she's not always lucid, due we assume, to the drugs she's taking. So…'

Sophie frowned and sighed. ' Okay, let' go back over what we do know. Victor Blanchet was the *notaire* who dealt with the purchase of Geraldine's house. Payments were being made to Geraldine after she moved into the house by the same *notaire*, Victor Blanchet. You suspect blackmail because of the amount of money and the fact that the payments continued after the house purchase.'

I nodded. 'Of course, we're just guessing about the blackmail because Geraldine won't confirm it.'

'But it is feasible, '' she agreed.

'Geraldine had an affair with Victor Blanchet, which she has admitted, and we considered it possible that as he knew how important her friendship was with his wife, she would pay not have it out in the open.'

'But…' Sophie frowned.

'I know what you're going to say, and we considered that already. Apparently Marie's mother knew about his affairs but we're guessing she didn't know who the latest one was with.'

'Hm, it's weak don't you think? I mean as a motive for blackmail.'

I sighed. 'Yeah, I suppose it is.' I shook my head. 'I don't know if there is any real mystery here to be honest, but as we couldn't help Malarie with the investigation into Jacques' death nor help Geraldine with the investigation into Julien's death, we thought finding out about Marie's father was the best use of our time.'

'Because Marie wanted to know about how he died you mean?'

I shrugged, 'I suppose so. I mean we're even guessing at that too really. Just because Inspector Borné has a reputation for incompetence doesn't necessarily mean he was wrong about how Victor Blanchet died. Maybe he did just get drunk and fall down some steps.'

'On the other hand, if Victor Blanchet was blackmailing Geraldine and then died suddenly, his death could easily have been arranged to look like an accident, especially if he was known to like his drink. Of course, if that's the case, you do realise that we're not only finding out the truth about Victor Blanchet, but also putting Geraldine in the frame for murder.'

I nodded slowly, acknowledging the impact of her reasoning and beginning to wonder whether it was a mistake to delve into this mystery at all.

Sophie sighed and stood up. 'Well, keep me informed of any new info you come across.'

'Will do.' I got up to walk with her to her car.

*

Marie contacted me via WhatsApp that evening.

She reported that Inspector Maupetit had examined the case file into her father's death and claimed it lacked diligence. He'd told her that certain procedures weren't followed as they should have been.

'Really?' I gaped. 'Did he say what exactly the problems were?'

Marie shook her head. 'He just said there was missing information but as it happened so long ago there was nothing he could do about it.'

'Oh no!' I sighed in frustration.

Meanwhile Marie held up her hand. 'Wait, there's more. he suggested that there may be still older people living in the area who could remember the death and maybe I should ask them. So, I decided to start with Malarie who, although young, I thought she might have heard about Victor Blanchet. I didn't tell her why I was asking though, I just asked if she had heard about his death and described how he had been found. She said she didn't recall the name even though the family had lived in the village forever, but she did remember a rumour about someone who had been found dead in those circumstances and the death ruled as accidental. She said her father once said he didn't believe it was an accident because the man had a lot of enemies so plenty of people were glad to see the back of him.'

'So now we're getting somewhere!' I exclaimed trying to contain my excitement.

Marie nodded but her face remained serious. It occurred to me that in discovering her father had been a murder victim, which in itself would surely be upsetting, finding out that Geraldine could be a murderer would be even worse.

'Are you sure you want to continue with this Marie?' I asked warily voicing my fears.

She nodded. 'We've come this far; we might as well know the truth.'

'And if Geraldine was involved in his death?'

She shrugged, her eyes downcast.

'Anything new on the other investigations?' I asked with a forced cheeriness.

Marie looked glad of the change of subject. 'According to the Inspector, Julien was killed with a single knife wound.'

Unsure what to do with that information I nodded without comment.

'By the way, why did Inspector Maupetit take over from Borné?'

'Borné retired.' She said simply.

'Oh I see, so maybe he's going to take over in Ruffec full time then instead of Borné.'

Marie shook her head 'Oh no, I think Inspector Maupetit is moving to Nantes.'

'Oh?'

She nodded. 'Big promotion apparently.'

I raised my eyebrows but again changed tack. 'Any luck with Geraldine?'

'I've tried but she is still confused and last time I spoke to her she was rambling again. But, I think she was saying something about how she shouldn't have trusted him. When I asked her whether she meant the *notaire*, she said yes.'

'She said she shouldn't have trusted the *notaire*? So that means Victor Blanchet?' I stared, wide eyed. Finally we could be getting to the bottom of it all.

Marie shrugged. 'I suppose so.'

'No more mention of V.J.?'

She shook her head. 'Oh, nearly forgot to tell you. The Inspector questioned Malarie and I was able to overhear. He asked her whether there was anything her father had talked about or been concerned about just before he died. She told him he had been ranting about the fishing license.'

'And that was all?'

'Malarie also said her father was angry that she had chosen to work for the family, but he had not explained why. Oh and something about him telling her how the previous owner died earlier than expected,' she shrugged, looking puzzled. 'It didn't make a lot of sense.'

*

Despite feeling that I'd spent the whole day relaying information from one person to another, I continued by phoning Sophie to pass on Marie's news. The conversation was short as she and Andre, her husband, were about to leave the house for an evening out. Nevertheless, she listened patiently to the details and promised to give them some thought before proposing lunch the following day with Lesley and Di.

CHAPTER TWENTYONE

Sophie texted early the next morning to tell me she would pick both me and Lesley up around twelve thirty.

'So where are we off to?' Asked Lesley.

'I found out about a lovely little restaurant near *Cheffois*. Thought we'd try it out. We're meeting Di there.' Replied Sophie.

We arrived around twenty minutes later at a smart looking natural stone building. Gravel walkways surrounded it, lined with neatly trimmed shrubs, giving the appearance of being newly landscaped. Inside, on the ground floor, was a small shop selling fresh local produce. We bypassed this to follow Sophie as she led us up a curved polished wooden staircase to the restaurant above on a mezzanine floor. Waiting to be shown to our table we all took time to gaze around appreciatively at the tasteful décor; natural textures mixed with a neutral colour scheme which gave the room a relaxed and rustic feel but with simple clean lines making it feel contemporary.

After a smiling waitress took us to our table, she handed us menus and then was at pains to explain how it contained dishes made from locally sourced ingredients. We all smiled politely and expressed delight at the notion. After taking a few minutes to share our admiration of the setting, we ordered wine and food and settled down to discuss the matter at hand.

Sophie began by saying that she'd thought over the details of our chat the evening before and had focused on what I'd said about how Geraldine's house and grounds were so large, and how it was likely therefore to have been expensive. She, like me, had wondered how Geraldine could have afforded to buy it.

'It would certainly be an expensive property to buy at today's prices.' Remarked Di.

Sophie smiled at Di to acknowledge her words. 'What if V.J. wasn't initials? What if Geraldine is pronouncing it as vee jay but it's actually vee a jay?' She gazed at the group to check the reaction to her proposal.

Like the others, I was puzzled. 'Is that supposed to mean something?'

'V*iager* pronounced vee a jay is a type of real estate transaction. It's where a buyer pays the vendor a down payment which is much less than the market value of the property. Then they pay monthly payments for the rest of the vendor's life.'

'And how does the buyer benefit from that?' Questioned Lesley.

'When the vendor dies, the property ownership is transferred to the buyer.' Answered Sophie.

'Oh I see,' I nodded. 'So you think Geraldine was paying the owner of the property monthly payments which meant she didn't have to pay the full cost of the property.'

Di and Lesley nodded. 'Makes sense,' said Di, 'and would explain how she could afford it.'

'Oh I see, so it means the vendor, or seller, gets a lump sum plus something to live on each month.' Nodded Lesley.

I frowned. 'But how is this relevant?'

'Well, the buyer can save a lot of money if the vendor dies early.' Explained Sophie.

'And if the vendor lives a long time the buyer will be paying for a long time.' Di added wryly.

Sophie nodded in agreement, 'It's a gamble I agree, but usually the owners are quite old when they agree to this arrangement.'

'Well, from the paperwork we found, it looked like Geraldine was lucky enough to have moved into the house not long after she began making the regular payments. It means the owner must've died fairly soon after Geraldine's payments started so I'm guessing she must've been quite elderly and perhaps in ill health.' I nodded.

'The thing is, if you're found to know about the owner's health problems the agreement is null and void.'

My eyes widened as she spoke 'And the owner died earlier than expected according to Jacques!'

Di looked puzzled. 'Meaning what exactly?'

I ignored Di's question. 'And didn't want Malarie working at the house because of it!'

Di's face cleared suddenly. 'What! Are we actually saying Geraldine made sure the owner died earlier?'

Lesley looked shocked. 'Murdered her you mean?'

'Now *that* could be a reason for blackmail.' Continued Sophie staring at me with a look of triumph.

I stared back at her as I registered her train of thought. 'Because Geraldine knowing about the owner's health problem would be illegal and the transaction annulled.'

We all fell silent to consider Sophie's theory which was just as our entrées were placed in front of us, each of us peering across to view the food on each other's plates and marvelling at how inviting our food looked.

I pondered the way forward while taking a slice of *baguette* from the basket. 'I suppose now we have to try to find out about the circumstances of the previous owner's death.'

'We do indeed.' Nodded Sophie, an excited glint in her eye.

'I feel sorry for Marie,' said Lesley sullenly. 'First she finds out her father was likely to have been murdered and then we're going to suggest that her mother's dear friend is likely to be the murderer.'

Di, Sophie and I traded guilty looks.

'I mean,' began Di, 'could someone else have killed him? Didn't Jacques tell Malarie that Victor had lots of enemies?'

I nodded. 'It's a possibility. But what about the payments Geraldine was making to him? It certainly seems likely that he was blackmailing her, giving her a clear motive to get rid of him.'

Sophie nodded. 'You know, I'm thinking about Geraldine and how she rambles. Didn't you say she was mumbling about not trusting someone?'

'According to Marie, yes.'

Sophie looked thoughtful. 'So, what she could mean by that? Who couldn't she trust?'

'Someone she told about killing Victor maybe?' Asked Lesley.

Sophie shook her head. 'I'm thinking what if she didn't kill him, maybe the trust issue relates to something else.'

'Maybe the will?' Said Di.

Sophie looked thoughtful. 'But hasn't the will only recently become an issue? I mean if she's rambling about the past then it might be someone from her past that she couldn't trust.'

We fell silent once again, contemplating Sophie's words. Unfortunately no one felt able to offer any ideas.

By the time our main course arrived, we'd decided that as we'd reviewed all the information at our disposal and exhausted all ideas about motives and suspects, we should forget about it all and enjoy the rest of our meal.

The conversation lightened from that moment on and we found ourselves laughing and chatting as we usually did about anything and nothing. Thankfully no one brought up the subject of my possible return to the UK.

*

I telephoned Marie later that day to ask if she could question Malarie again. I wanted to find out if Malarie could recall what exactly Jacques had said about the previous house owner, specifically regarding the owner's health. Marie quizzed me about what I was trying to find out. Of course, as I didn't want her to know that I was trying to establish whether Geraldine had committed murder, I was evasive. 'I'm not sure how this all goes together yet.'

Marie was quiet for a moment and I suspected she was unhappy with my response but fortunately, she didn't persist.

'I had breakfast with Geraldine this morning and she seemed quite lucid. She even opened up about a few things.'

'Oh?'

'She apologized to me for the affair with my father, not that she needed to of course but she explained that she broke it off with him when she found out he was married. She met Henri soon after and about the same time found out she was pregnant. She decided it was in her best interests to allow Henri to believe the child was his. We spoke for a while before she began to ramble on again about not trusting the *notaire*.'

'So she specified the *notaire* as the person she didn't trust? That is, she didn't trust Victor Blanchet, your father?' I repeated, trying to work out if there were any implications from this extra piece of information. 'I think so,' said Marie, 'even though she often seems to talk about the *notaire* and my father as if they were different people.'

'Hm, strange. Did she say anything else?'

'Just something about it not being her fault.'

'Not her fault…' my voice trailed off. Could she mean Victor's death wasn't her fault? Or could she mean the house owner's death wasn't her fault? I thought it prudent to keep both thoughts to myself and didn't respond.

'Cat'rine?'

'Yes, still here. I was thinking, next time you talk to Geraldine, see if she knows anything about a *viager* arrangement.'

'*Viager*?'

'Yes, Sophie came up with an interesting idea about Geraldine's purchase of the house and wondered if she'd entered into this type of arrangement. She thinks it could be vee a jay, the arrangement, rather than V.J. being a person.'

'Oh!' Said Marie sounding surprised. 'That's an idea!'

We chatted a while longer about how Geraldine was coping with her medication. Then Marie disclosed that she'd rekindled her friendship with Hugo, and we ended the call.

I received an SMS text from Marie a few hours later. It simply said, 'yes, Geraldine bought the house using the *viager* arrangement.'

*

While washing dishes my thoughts turned involuntarily to Inspector Borné. I wondered if he'd investigated the house owner's death and if so what conclusion he came to. I thought about how he'd ruled Victor's death as an accident. Was he just incompetent as we thought, or could there be something else going on? Victor Blanchet supposedly had lots of enemies. Could the Inspector have been one of them? Could he have botched the investigation because it suited him? But why? What possible connection could there have been between Victor Blanchet and Inspector Borné? I shook my head as if to physically shake it out my mind and went to change for dinner with Tim and Lesley.

Marie phoned as I was about to leave. I could tell by her voice that her earlier optimism had waned. She reported that Malarie was now reluctant to answer any more questions and hadn't been to the house recently anyway as she was no longer needed now that the family had all gone. Collette, however, was still in contact with Malarie and told Marie that Malarie was angry that no one had yet been arrested for her father's murder. Marie also complained that Inspector Maupetit had refused to find out the circumstances around the previous house owner's death, telling her most emphatically that he would not spend time investigating a death from years ago when he was busy trying to investigate two murders from recent weeks. She said she thought Inspector Maupetit was annoyed because he'd only been allowed a limited time to solve both cases and now had less manpower due to officers being taken from him. I agreed with her notion that the Inspector was probably peeved because he was working with limited time and budget.

CHAPTER TWENTYTWO

Tim led me through to the dining room where Lesley and Monsieur Lagard were already seated at the table, wine flowing.

'Ah Madame Patterson,' the *maire* stood up to greet me, kissing on both cheeks. I took a seat opposite Lesley just as Tim promptly brought in an *hors d'oeuvres* starter, placing a small dish of tapenade with a slice of crusty bread in front of each of us.

'Ooh looks delicious. Karl will be sorry to have missed it.' I smiled apologetically.

'He was offered a job in the UK I hear.' Said Monsieur Lagard. Straight to the point, I noted. 'Yes,' I tried to maintain a cheery smile. He nodded, studying my face, 'And Aidan? He is enjoying his new life?'

'Loving it,' I smiled. 'Last time we spoke he was going to organize a dig in the Scottish Highlands.'

The *maire* smiled ruefully in response.

'Dig in!' Advised Tim, sensing the conversation was about to become sombre.

The *maire* picked up his cutlery. '*Alors*, Ruffec!' He glanced from me to Lesley with a cheery expression. 'How did you find it?'

'I enjoyed it. If we hadn't been focusing on finding out information for our host…'

'Ah *oui*, Madame Dupont. I have heard about this from Sophie.'

I nodded, realizing he probably knew everything that we did.

The *maire* paused to take a sip of wine. 'You know during the second world war Ruffec was at the centre of *la Résistance* for the evacuation of Allied airmen toward Spain.'

'Oh really?'

'*Oui*, you may have heard of the Cockleshell heroes?'

I shrugged and glanced at Lesley who was looking puzzled. 'Afraid not.'

The *maire* looked surprised. 'I believe they made a film about them?'

'Oh yes, think I might've seen that.' Said Tim, standing up to clear away our dishes.

'I'd love to hear about that,' said Lesley.

The *maire* smiled, watching Tim leave the room. 'I'll wait until chef has rejoined us.'

The conversation turned to a recent weather forecast predicting stormy weather.

'Oh yes, supposed to be gale force winds,' nodded Lesley, a grave look on her face.

The *maire* nodded. 'I'm hoping we don't have a problem with power cables like the last time.'

'Oh yes,' I nodded, 'I remember the whole area was affected.'

Just then Tim returned to place a large dish of *Tartiflette* on the table together with a large tomato and onion salad.

After expressing delight and complimenting Tim on the presentation of his dishes, we helped ourselves. The flattery of Tim continued while we ate with both the *maire* and me declaring the food to be delicious. Once we'd had our fill and settled back into our seats, Monsieur Lagard began his tale.

'Now then, the Cockleshell heroes.'

We all gave the *maire* our full attention, waiting patiently.

'It was in December nineteen forty two when ten British Royal Marine Commandoes carried out Operation Frankton.'

'Oh!' Remarked Lesley, trying to show polite interest.

The *maire* nodded, smiling. 'They were trained for the operation in two-man canoes off the Hampshire coast.'

'Ah yes,' interrupted Tim, 'wasn't it the name of the canoe which gave them their nickname?'

The *maire* nodded, looking pleased. '*Oui monsieur*, the canoes were Cockle Mark II canoes, a type of folding kayak.' He took a sip of wine. 'They set off from Portsmouth on a submarine named HMS Tuna.'

Lesley chuckled. 'Great name for a submarine.'

The *maire* smiled politely at the interruption before continuing. 'Their mission was to attack the enemy German cargo ships moored at the port of Bordeaux in occupied France.'

I listened, fascinated.

'The team, launched from the submarine to travel behind enemy lines. They could only travel by night to avoid being seen, and of course, evade capture.' He paused and glanced around to confirm everyone was captured by his story.

Lesley took a sip of wine. 'How far did they have to travel in a tiny canoe?'

'It was said to be ninety-seven *kilométres*, or sixty miles. They had to paddle down the Gironde estuary with the aim of infiltrating Bordeaux harbour.'

'So daring!' Remarked Tim.

The *maire* nodded. '*En effet*, Monsieur.'

I was keen to know how exactly they were meant to carry out their task, but I knew Monsieur Lagard considered himself something of a raconteur and didn't like to be rushed through his story telling. Lesley had no qualms, however.

'How on earth could they attack cargo ships in little canoes?' She asked, almost in disbelief.

I spotted a brief flash of irritation cross the *maire's* face but being too polite to complain of the interruption, he simply smiled. 'They were tasked with attaching limpet mines to the German ships.'

'And were they successful?' I asked, suddenly impatient.

He nodded. 'Six enemy ships were successfully damaged.'

'But they didn't all escape if I remember rightly.' Added Tim.

'Alas *non*,' the *maire* conceded. 'Only two survived the raid.'

'Oh no!' Exclaimed Lesley looking shocked.

The *maire* nodded sadly. 'Six were executed by the Germans and two died from hypothermia.'

Lesley looked amazed. 'So two of them made it to Ruffec?'

He nodded. 'Indeed, they escaped inland to Ruffec and from there, members of the French Resistance guided them across the Pyrenees and onto Gibraltar. They were then able to leave for the UK.'

'What a tale to tell your grandchildren!' Exclaimed Tim.

'Do you know their names?' Enquired Lesley curiously.

'Bill Sparks and Herbert Hassler.' Responded the *maire* without hesitation.

I shook my head, amazed at his memory for details.

Tim suddenly brought the conversation to an end with his announcement of sticky toffee pudding for dessert. It was met with squeals of delight when he also produced a large jug of custard to go with it. The mood was once again animated and while the *maire* quizzed Tim about ingredients he'd used for the dishes we'd enjoyed, Lesley enlightened me with details about her grandchildren and when they would be returning to France.

As the evening drew to an end, I felt saddened, wondering how many more dinners with friends I had left to enjoy before leaving France.

*

I tossed and turned that night unable to shake the guilty feeling that we'd more or less overlooked the threat to Geraldine's life. Dismissing her fears just because no one could corroborate the story of the poisoned cat and the notes. Shouldn't we have spent more time on this? And now, having discovered she may have been involved in a murder, was the threat any less serious? I pondered the family members as possible perpetrators. Neither Di, Marie nor I had found the family, with the exception of Julien, to be anything other than pleasant. Could we condemn some of them for making clandestine

searches of Geraldine's room for a will? Assuming that is what they were after of course, we had no proof that was the case. It was just that it came up so much in conversation, it seemed the likeliest reason.
I got up to fetch a glass of water. My mind whirling with 'what if' scenarios. Geraldine had admitted to us that she'd used the idea of a will to lure everyone to her home. Maybe I should suggest to Marie that she ask Geraldine whether she has a will. She'd already told us that Henri didn't. Were the family aware of Geraldine's will? If it was a will according to UK law, who were the beneficiaries? Would that have any bearing on their furtive behaviour?
I lay down again trying to sleep but still couldn't shake the nagging feeling at the back of my mind about the way the family had not discussed Julien's murder. His name had not even been mentioned after his death. I tried to recall the meals we'd had together since his demise and struggled to bring to mind any of the family looking grief stricken. Had the rancour we'd witnessed between Julien and some of his siblings meant they were all glad to see him dead? Their own brother? An even more menacing thought crossed my mind. Did they choose not to speak of him because they were *all* involved in his death? Or did they know the murderer was one of them and were closing ranks?

TWENTYTHREE

I had intimated to Lesley at dinner the previous evening that I had news but, not wanting to bring down the mood, had invited her for coffee the next day instead to bring her up to date.
'So Marie's been in touch again? I'm guessing about information on her father.' She said taking a bite out of an éclair.

I nodded taking the seat opposite. 'Unfortunately she can't ask Inspector Maupetit for any help with anything that happened in the past because he's refused to investigate anything other than Jacques and Julien's murder.'

She raised her eyebrows. 'And have the police got any suspects yet?'

I shook my head. 'I think the police are going round in circles to be honest. No one saw or heard anything the night Julien was killed. They can't place anyone from the wine scam, the few they know about that is, at the scene, and there just doesn't seem to be any other motive. Similarly with Jacques. No one saw or heard anything. Though…'

'Yes?'

I sighed. 'Well it did cross my mind that the family could have murdered one or both of them and were putting on a united show of ignorance. Farfetched I know.'

Lesley looked sceptical. 'Motive?'

I shrugged.

'Is that your notepad?' She nodded toward it on the table.

'Yeah, was looking through it just before you came.'

Lesley took a gulp of coffee. 'Ok, why don't we think up a list of reasons why people murder. It might prove useful.'

'Good idea,' I said with and mouthful of éclair. Picking up my pen I searched for a clean page. 'Ready,' I said, moving a plate out of the way.

'Jealousy,' Lesley offered.

I nodded. 'Greed, as in a robbery maybe.'

'Or greed as in 'that's my inheritance, not yours',’

We exchanged a brief meaningful look.

'Blackmail.' She suggested, no doubt thinking about Geraldine's situation.

'Revenge.' I added, writing furiously.

Lesley nodded, 'That must feature a lot I reckon.'

'How about witnessing a crime?'

'Hm,' She nodded. 'Or even *knowing* about something. I mean you could be murdered if it's something someone doesn't want you to know about.'

I stared at her suddenly. 'What if Jacques knew something? He claimed to know something about Geraldine and her family that no one else did.'

'You mean knowing about the owner dying earlier than expected?'

I nodded, 'and he must have suspected Geraldine for having something to do with it which is why he didn't want Malarie working there.'

'So, he blamed Geraldine with her motive being she would benefit by getting the house.' She nodded. 'Yeah, I can understand his reasoning. So, do you think she could've killed Jacques? I mean if she didn't want anyone finding out.'

'Geraldine? No, no. Cast iron alibi. And anyway, why *now*? If she did murder the previous owner and believed Jacques knew about it, wouldn't she have tried to do something about it years ago?'

'I suppose.'

I shook my head. 'The problem is we're still just guessing and no one's any closer to any motive for the recent murders.'

I gazed down at the list in front of me and took a sip of coffee.

'What about revenge? Maybe someone wanted revenge for killing the owner or killing the *notaire*?'

I shrugged. 'Again I'm wondering why *now*? I mean your guess is as good as mine but if it's revenge, as you say, I would plump for someone trying to avenge the house owner. I mean, I doubt Victor Blanchet was even missed since he was reported to have had so many enemies.'

'What if someone has just recently found out what Geraldine did to the owner and is now out to exact revenge? Perhaps they didn't know about it at the time?'

I shook my head. 'Hang on, I think we've lost our focus. Revenge for Geraldine killing the owner wouldn't lead to someone murdering Jacques or Julien. From this line of reasoning, Geraldine would be the only one with a motive for killing Jacques because he knew too much. And we know she didn't do it.'
Lesley looked disappointed. 'It's a real headscratcher isn't it?'
I agreed as we both finished off our eclairs and I refilled our cups.

*

I was alone that evening after a call from Karl. He'd told me he only needed to be in the UK for a few more days and was going to check the flights to see if he could arrange to be back for the weekend. It would be good to get back to normal I mused, though I didn't relish explaining how I was once again mixed up in finding murderers and someone threatening Geraldine's life. Knowing Karl preferred me to run our business without causing the police to be at our door every other day, made me dread the conversation.

Thinking back to the list of motives I'd cowritten with Lesley and which had given us some new ideas, I decided that writing down a list of all possible suspects and trying to rule them out one by one would make sense. No doubt the Inspector had already done that as a matter of course, but since he usually didn't share all of his information, instead preferring to drip feed me details so he could coax me into revealing everything I knew, it would help to organize my thoughts. Everyone's background needed looking into I decided. We hadn't managed to find out anything about the family's circumstances other than who was married or divorced and the children they had. And that information had come from Geraldine herself. We'd never actually found out anything extra, like what they did for a living or how they liked to spend their leisure time. Our focus had, rightly or wrongly, simply been on behaviour exhibited toward Geraldine and whether it could be classed as suspicious. It made me feel rather ashamed at how remiss we'd been, considering how we'd been tasked to discover information.

We did know however, that some of the family had been snooping in Geraldine's bedroom, presumably for the will, though what else did we have? We'd found the family, except for Julien and to some extent, Genevieve, to be perfectly amiable.

So what about others in the household? I wrote down each name, making rough notes about each one.

There didn't seem to be any reason for Collette to harm Geraldine. She'd been with Geraldine for several years and had only moved to the area just before that. What possible motive could she have?

Malarie might be resentful on behalf of her father because he couldn't get the fishing license but was that a strong enough motive to do someone harm?

How about the Dutch gardener, Aldert? We didn't know anything about him but surely the Inspector would've checked him out.

Should the doctor be in this mix of suspects? Someone the family claimed had gone out of his way to help them. They were all so grateful to him and said that he'd looked after Henri when he'd had his heart attack. They had full confidence in him.

Sighing in frustration, mostly at my inability to come up with any plausible motives, I closed the notebook and went to make a cup of tea.

Sophie telephoned that evening and before she had a chance to speak I put to her the theory of revenge.

'If it is a question of revenge,' she replied thoughtfully, 'maybe we should search for someone who would *want* revenge.'

'Hm, check out their alibi or even rule that person out as a suspect you mean.'

'Which would also be useful to rule it out as a motive.' She paused. 'By the way, the reason I called was to let you know I've been checking some old newspaper reports and found the report on the previous owner's death.'

'Great!' I interrupted.

'Well, no, not really. It was reported that there were no suspicious circumstances so there wasn't a post-mortem. Apparently the family knew she had health problems.'

'Oh!' I couldn't help but reveal my disappointment.

'However,' she continued. 'There was a paragraph which stated that family members refused to believe the cause of death because they said she'd lived with a heart problem for many years and took good care of herself because of it, meaning her death was still unexpected. They also requested a post-mortem but it was refused.'

I sighed audibly.

'Maybe it's worth trying to get in touch with someone from the family, see what else they knew?' She said kindly, trying to alleviate my disappointment.

'You know, I've begun to wonder whether we should even be bothering to dig up the past.' I said gloomily.

'How so?' Asked Sophie.

'Well, all we seem to be doing is putting Geraldine in the frame as a murder suspect.'

'Hm, I suppose for Marie it means finding out the truth of what happened to her father. Give her some closure, as the Americans say. And then I suppose we could leave it up to her whether she wants to disclose what was found out to the police.'

'Yes that's a good idea,' I replied, a little more upbeat. 'So, now to find someone related to the previous owner.'

'Well, I have already looked into that.'

'Wow, Sophie, you're so efficient!'

She chuckled. 'Well, I envisaged our conversation heading in this direction. So, it seems there is a nephew still alive. His mother, the owner's sister, now dead, was actually on record for accusing Geraldine of killing the owner.'

My mouth dropped open her news. 'No!'

'Oh yes, *and*,' she paused for dramatic effect, 'the nephew most conveniently, works in a laboratory near Ruffec. He apparently started working there after moving up from the south coast around four months ago. The lab is in a local clinic and his name is Gabriel Badeau.'

'Sophie you're a star!' I interjected as I jotted down his name.

'Could be worth talking to him to see if he can remember anything about it.' She added cheerily.

'Absolutely!'

CHAPTER TWENTYFOUR

The next morning I checked online for the phone number of a clinic close to Ruffec and telephoned straightaway. A woman answered the phone and I asked for Monsieur Badeau. She informed me there was a laboratory technician named Badeau so would put me through to the other line.

'*Allo?*'

When a male voice answered I told him my name and again asked if I could speak to Monsieur Badeau.

'*Oui, C'est moi. Qu'est-ce que tu veux?*'

'I'm trying to find out what happened to Emilie Vidale, who I believe was your mother's sister. She died many years ago.'

'*Oui*' He sounded wary.

I tried to sound cheerful, better to keep him on side so he felt able to talk to me, perhaps we could even meet to discuss what he knew. 'It could have some bearing on a recent investigation if you could tell me anything you remember.'
He was silent.
'Monsieur?'
'*Je suis ici*,'
I assumed he needed more information before making a decision. 'I believe your mother made accusations against the current owner of your aunt's house, implying she was somehow complicit in her death.'
'*Et vous etes impliqué dans l'enquete?*'
I replied that yes, I was involved in the investigation.
'*Encore ton nom?*'
I reminded him of my name.
There was a few more moments of silence before he spoke.
'Are you the woman who helps the *gendarmes* with their investigations? I've seen you in the newspaper. You own a *chambres d'hotes* in the Deux Sevres.'
'That's right,' he was getting distracted and I needed to steer him back to my questioning.
'*Oui, peut etre nous pouvons rencontrer ?*'
Yes, I said, maybe it would be better to meet so I could find out everything he knew. He told me he would check his diary and get back in touch with me so I read out my phone number. He thanked me and said that I would be hearing from him soon.
Struck dumb, as if in some sort of daydream, I opened my mouth to reply but no sound came out. Suddenly aware that I'd become debilitated by a growing sense of unease now developing rapidly into one of dread made me stutter some incomprehensible response.
'Madame?'

From out of the enveloping haziness, I managed to create the wherewithal to pretend that I was suddenly being called away. I hurriedly ended the call. Glancing down I found my hands were shaking.

I sat staring into space for several minutes, my heart racing. I needed to think. Think Catherine! How did this all fit together? It was imperative I spoke to Inspector Maupetit. He would make sense of it. Quickly, I searched for his stored number on my mobile then waited impatiently for him to pick up. Unfortunately, after several vain attempts I was forced to leave a message. Conscious of having only a limited time to speak, I raced through my news. I told him that I'd phoned the nephew of Emily Vidale, explaining she was the previous owner of Geraldine's house, and that as I was speaking to him I'd realised that Geraldine was in great danger. I also hurriedly said that if I was correct then that same person posing the danger could have a motive for murdering Jacques, but I needed to check some details first. I paused briefly, wondering how much more I could say but decided to finish by saying that I still hadn't connected all the dots and asked if he could return my call as it was a matter of utmost urgency. Annoyingly, his voicemail cut off before I had time to say more just as I was regretting ending the call with a metaphor.

I fretted for several more minutes before deciding to phone Marie. A short while later and still no reply, I telephoned Geraldine's house. Collette answered. She told me that Geraldine's condition had worsened and after having no luck trying to get hold of the doctor she'd been taken to hospital. Marie had gone with her. We agreed that Marie had probably turned off her mobile. After ending the call I stared at my phone. Geraldine had believed her life was in danger and she'd been right. And now she was fighting for her life. We'd let her down.

I hated sitting waiting for the phone to ring so I resolved to use up my nervous energy by keeping myself busy. Emptying and cleaning the kitchen cupboards had been on my to do list for a long time but kept finding its way to the bottom, so I decided now was as good a time as any. It would take my mind off things.

Twenty minutes later and the kitchen looked like a bomb site, but I was engrossed in my task. A low rumble of thunder distracted me for a moment making me notice how gloomy the kitchen had become due no doubt to the darkening sky outside. Going to flick on the light, I recalled the weather forecast about the coming storm but my mind strayed. Why hadn't the Inspector returned my call? Didn't he think my message was important enough to respond? Maybe he hadn't understood because what I'd said because it was too garbled.

I rang him again. No response. Sighing in frustration I decided my message needed to be more urgent. So, after the beep I pleaded. 'Please get in touch! It's vitally important I speak to you!' I ended the call. That should do it. Now I just had to hope he wasn't going to refute all the details, motives and suspects from my theory and be annoyed that I'd dragged him away from his work to phone me.

Suddenly my phone rang. I snatched it up, an unknown caller.
'*Allo?*'
No one replied, yet I felt sure that someone was on the other end of the line.
'*Allo?*' I repeated feeling my panic rise. Still no answer so I ended the call. I couldn't waste time, I needed to be ready to take a call from the Inspector or Marie.

CHAPTER TWENTYFIVE

I glanced outside. The wind was really picking up. Surveying the garden for a moment, I watched the trees bending and arching as the wind grew fiercer. When large spots of rain splashed to the ground I was finally spurred into action. Throwing on a coat, I hurried outside to batten down the hatches, while hearing another low rumble of thunder as I dragged the shutters closed. In the failing light, I pulled up the hood of my coat to protect me from the now torrential rain and moved around to the other side of the house to close the rest of the shutters. There was a flicker of lightning just as I went to push open the front door, but I was suddenly forced to a halt, listening. Was that a banging sound coming from the barn? My shoulders sagged. Oh no. I had no option but to go and secure the building otherwise whatever door or shutter was banging would be making a racket all night. Hurrying across the garden I couldn't help but stare in alarm as I approached the barn. Was that the lightning outside, lighting up the inside? No one had been in the barn since Karl had left for England a few weeks back. I sincerely hoped the bursts of illumination weren't coming from an electric light that had been left on all that time.
Once I reached the barn, I moved the usual 'doorstop' rock to jam open the front door; I didn't want it banging while I was inside searching for the offending light. A light that was now flickering erratically, giving the place a distinctly eerie look.
Taking a moment to scan the large open room, I noticed the area beneath the mezzanine was lit up so went across to flip the switch. Just then the light flickered again before going off completely. A loud rumble of thunder was accompanied by another flash of lightning. The room lit up the room again, this time just long enough for me to catch a glimpse of a figure looming toward me. Catching sight of a glint of steel in his hand, I gasped, stumbling back in terror. Feeling my back hit against a countertop I was horrified to discover I was trapped. When the light flickered on again, I came face to face with my

assailant and braced myself, waiting to feel the pain of the knife plunging into me.

'So *the* Catherine Patterson.' Unexpectedly, the man halted just steps away.

Taking a deep breath, I forced myself to look at him and somehow found the courage to speak. A bold thought of talking him out of his murderous course of action flittered through my mind and made me pull myself up tall.

'We…we were never formally introduced Doctor, or should I call you Gabriel?' I swallowed, my mouth dry.

His lip curled into a sneer. 'Monsieur Badeau will do.'

'Why are you here, er, Monsieur Badeau? I mean what…what do you want?'

He looked amused, clearly enjoying watching me squirm, while taking his time to reply. After a few moments he took his gaze to the knife he was holding, touching the blade with his fingers to check the sharpness. 'Before we go any further, I want some answers.'

'I'm not sure if I know…' I began.

'Oh *ça suffit!* Madame, you know far too much.' His face took on a malevolent look. 'I want to know how you worked it out. How you knew it was me?'

'I… I didn't, I thought you wanted to meet…'

'Don't lie to me!' He snarled. 'I knew you realized it was me when we spoke on the phone. You gave yourself away by your reaction to what I said. I heard the panic in your voice when you ended the call.' He mocked. 'You know, you're not a very good actor at all.'

Gripped by fear but running on adrenalin, I realised trying to deny it was useless. Maybe if I told him what he needed, he might leave without me coming to harm. I grimaced. Stop kidding yourself Catherine!

'Your voice…er…accent.' I stuttered. 'I recognised it from when I heard you speaking at Geraldine Dupont's house. I…I knew that how you spoke, that was…. Coming from Marseille, you had a very distinct accent.'

He stared at me in amazement.

'And…er, I was trying to work out if someone was threatening Geraldine's life for something she did in her past. So…when I spoke to you on the phone, I realised who you were, and I put two and two together. Emilie Vidale's nephew, pretending to be Geraldine's doctor, someone who had recently moved back into the area. Yes, that's it!' I'd been speculating for so long but now had a sudden moment of clarity. 'You wanted revenge because you thought, as your mother did, that Geraldine had killed your aunty to take her house.'

He scoffed. 'You think that's all there was to it? *Tellement stupide!* I thought the *great* Catherine Patterson would be able to come up with something better than that.'

He shifted position and I instinctively jerked backward. Expecting that I had nothing more to offer I frantically tried to extend our conversation.

'*Please*,' I begged. 'Why don't you tell me where I've gone wrong? Tell me your side the story.'

He looked at me thoughtfully, weighing up my words before glancing upward in response to a large clap of thunder and the sound of heavy rain hitting the barn roof.

'*Eh bien*, since I am in no hurry to leave, I will humour you.' He folded his arms, the knife still in his hand, and moved a few steps away to lean casually against a nearby wall.

'I'm guessing in your search you have come across the name Victor Blanchet?'

I nodded.

'This *worm*,' he almost spat the word out, 'befriended my mother. He was her world; she would tell me later. At the time she lived with her sister, Emilie in the house that now belongs to Geraldine Dupont. When my mother became pregnant, Victor wanted no more to do with her. Accusing her of being unfaithful and saying the child wasn't his. But not only that, he then turned his attentions to Emilie, the older sister. She was no doubt flattered that a man nearly fifteen years her junior was interested in her. But he wasn't interested in her, not really. *Non*, he simply made it his business to turn Emilie against her sister, *ma mère*.'

Gabriel's face was stony as he recalled the story, but his voice remained calm. 'Then Emilie turned my mother out of the house.'

'But who owned it?' I asked, temporarily forgetting my fear.

'Both owned it, both inherited it from their parents.' He replied.

I stared at him in confusion.

'I presume you know Victor Blanchet was a *notaire*?'

I nodded.

'Well, he made sure, through illicit means, that Emilie had all the legal documents to show that the house was solely in her name. My mother was left with nothing. Nowhere to live, no property to her name and a child on the way.'

Despite myself I began to feel pity for this man in front of me.

'*Bien entendu*, Victor wasn't interested in Emilie, He was interested in the house and how to get his hands on it. Of course, he couldn't marry Emilie because he already had a wife.'

I nodded, registering that he was referring to Marie's mother.

'When Geraldine Dupont came along, looking for a place to live and being someone who could easily be duped into this *viager* arrangement for buying a house, he was set. All he had to do was get Emilie to agree to it and then arrange for Emilie's death. No one would question it because she already had a heart condition. Then on her death,

Madame Dupont would acquire a home. Between the two of them, Victor and Madame Dupont had managed to obtain a property for buttons. Property which today, I guess, would be valued at about two or three million euros.'

'But how do you know Geraldine was involved? I mean, couldn't she have been an innocent party?'

A flicker of uncertainty crossed Gabriel Badeau's face before being transformed into a hard look. '*Non*, I don't believe she would have willingly gone into this agreement without knowing about Emilie's illness. Emilie wasn't an old woman which meant payments under *viager* were more likely to have gone on for years. Most people only go into this arrangement when the house owner is much older.'

'Yes, I see.'

'*Et puis*, you came along,' He pushed himself off the wall.

'But wait, *please*, tell me,' I gave him a pleading look. 'Why *now*? Why wait all this time to do something about it?'

'*La chance? La destinée?*' He said with a shrug. 'I had just moved back to the area. I became a temporary part of SAMU, an assistant in the emergency team which was called to Geraldine Dupont's house when she became ill. Realising who she was and knowing what had happened to my mother and how that property should have been passed down to me, filled me with rage. I had to do something about it.'

'But you work in a lab, you're not actually a doctor?' I asked incredulously.

His lip curled derisively. 'I have some medical training, not sufficient to qualify as a doctor but, enough to fool you and her family.'

'And so you *pretended* to be her doctor,' I said, almost to myself.

'Correct!' He said gleefully. 'And,' he sighed now as if bored. 'I've had to make myself available, to be at Madame's beck and call while I administered drugs and potions.' He rolled his eyes. 'Anything to make sure no one knew who I was or what I was up to. Of course, the family didn't have much interest anyway. All those children, and no one who cared enough to question her medical treatment.'

His argument struck a chord as I recalled only once hearing one of her children asking about Geraldine's treatment, and that was only when they were about to leave.

I gave him a puzzled look. 'Are you saying that Geraldine is not terminally ill? That you've been giving her drugs which have caused her illness and confusion?'

He nodded, smirking. 'I needed to make her pay for what she did. And of course, as part of her gratitude, she has recently decided to name me as main beneficiary in her will.'

'Her French will?' I asked sceptically.

He looked pleased with himself. 'Ah *non*, of course not. I couldn't get the house that way. *Non*, her English will, recognised in French law for a UK citizen, so she can choose anyone she wants to inherit.'

My mouth dropped open. So Gabriel Badeau, also known as 'the doctor' had been ingratiating himself to Geraldine. Persuading her that he should benefit when she was gone.

'And you encouraged her to accuse her own family of trying to kill her?' I gasped.

He laughed suddenly. 'Clever plan isn't it? Of course, I needed to try it out, see how easy it was to get her to turn against her own flesh and blood.'

'So you killed her cat?' I was guessing at what he meant.

He gave me an admiring look. '*Oh la la*! Aren't we the smart one?'

'What I don't understand is how come there was another cat which the family…'

'…believed was the same cat.' He finished. 'Yes, a stroke of genius on my part I think. I had to produce a dead cat so was forced to kill a similar looking one and persuade Madame Dupont that it was hers. I also produced a threatening note which conveniently went missing as well as some other crude note which was of no importance but of course Madame Dupont was, with drugs and illness becoming very suggestible. I can't actually believe how easy it was to get her to turn on her own family.'

'So Jacques didn't confirm that the cat had been poisoned?'

He rolled his eyes. '*Oui bien sur*, but that's an altogether other story.' He took a step toward me making my heart thud in panic.

'Which I would love to hear! Help me understand, *please*.' I blurted out hastily.

He studied me for a moment, no doubt guessing at my delaying tactics but now unable to resist confessing all, enjoying how superior it made him feel.

'*D'accord*,' he moved to lean back against the wall again. 'Jacques asked if I could help persuade Madame Dupont to grant him a fishing license. He said he would owe me a favour, which I immediately called in. I told him that he needed to confirm that the cat, her cat, had been poisoned. Of course, he thought it was odd but he went along with it in accordance with our agreement. Then, when I told him she still refused to give him the license, he became angry and threatened to expose the lie. I couldn't let him do that. It would destroy my plan before I'd even begun.'

'So you killed him?' My voice was not much more than a whisper.

He shrugged. 'It had to be done.'

'So it was nothing to do with the past?'

'*Le passé?*'

'I thought Jacques knew too much and that was why he was killed. You see, I think he knew Emilie Vidale had been killed unlawfully and that Geraldine, Madame Dupont, was responsible. I also thought your motive for murdering him was because he recognised you as Emilie

Vidale's nephew. How wrong I was! And then you killed him, not knowing he was actually on your side!'

Gabriel Badeau looked momentarily confused while he processed my words, swallowing as if finding the information hard to digest.

'*C'est n'importe*. He was still in the way.' He said casually, though his expression was pained. Was he just realising that Jacques could have been a useful ally in this whole saga?

'And Julien?' I persisted, not knowing if any of this could have any bearing on Julien's death.

'Ah, *quel idiot*! For some reason he had done some research on Victor Blanchet. He claimed to know that Victor was the *notaire* who dealt with the purchase of his mother's house." He paused momentarily to ponder before speaking as if to himself. 'So, Jacques must have told him about his mother, Madame Dupont, killing Emilie and how no one even suspected anyone else was to blame for Emilie's death. He must have told Julien about it because he knew of Julien's resentment toward his mother,' he paused again, looking thoughtful then finally, as if making a decision he said, '*de toute facon*, Julien's research led him to a photograph of Emilie and her family. He showed it to me and told me that he knew who I was.'

It occurred to me at that moment, that his resemblance to Julien must have also given him away. 'So you killed him?' I asked incredulously. He raised an eyebrow. 'I killed him because he wanted money – a lot of money to buy his silence.'

The rain had eased but I could still hear low rumbles of thunder in the distance as my mind raced, frantically trying to make sense of it all. 'The rose garden,' I began.

Gabriel looked surprised for a moment before shaking his head. '*Quel erreur!* If I had been quicker, I could have killed you then. All this,' he made a sweeping movement with his arm, the knife in his hand coming eerily into focus, 'would not have been necessary.'

'So it was you who lured me there,' I said almost to myself.

'*Et maintenant*,' said Gabriel taking a step toward me 'I need to tie up more loose ends.'

'I know why Julien was researching Victor.' I said hastily.

He halted in his tracks, waiting for me to continue.

'Victor…was his father too,' I said.

Self-doubt momentarily crossed his face but he shrugged it off.

'*Suffisant*!' He snarled.

I braced myself as he moved closer, panicking that I had nothing at hand with which to even try to defend myself.

'*Police*! *Put the knife down!*'

I jumped suddenly at the sound of Sergeant Laurent's voice from behind, my heart pounding. Venturing to turn away from Gabriel who was gazing at the officer with a stunned expression, I caught sight of the handgun pointed at Gabriel. With a mixture of both shock and relief I stood frozen to the spot.

Gabriel, realising the game was up, immediately lifted his hands in surrender, loosening his hold on the knife and about to drop it. Suddenly there was a loud clap of thunder. The lights flickered then went off. In that instant I was grabbed roughly, one arm gripping me tightly while the other held the point of the knife to my neck. The light flickered on again. I was now facing Sergeant Laurent, my back against Gabriel. His trembling breath loud against my ear as he made this his desperate attempt to flee.

'Drop your gun officer, or Madame Catherine Patterson here has come to the end of her sleuthing career.'

Hesitating for a moment before throwing me an apologetic glance, Sergeant Laurent reluctantly bent down to place his gun on the ground. He then took a step forward, his hands lifted in a plea to Gabriel.

'Just let her go and we can talk,' he coaxed.

Gabriel took a step back automatically, dragging me along with him.

'No further!'

The officer heeded the warning and stood stock still, his hands still raised.

'I've had enough talking,' Gabriel said as he moved a few steps sideways toward the door forcing me to shuffle with him as his grip tightened.

'You don't need to do this,' the officer tried again, his voice gentle. Gabriel's grip intensified but he didn't reply, simply continuing to shuffle sideways toward the open doorway.

Suddenly there was the sound of a click. 'Don't give me a reason to shoot.' Inspector Maupetit's voice was calm and controlled.

Gabriel's grip loosened instantly and the knife clattered to the ground. Released from my restraint, I rushed forward to escape. Turning as soon as I felt safe to take a step backward and watching as Gabriel Badeau fell to his knees with his hands in the air. The Inspector holstered his handgun before pulling Gabriel's arms behind his back and forcing handcuffs onto his wrists. He glanced up at me briefly before pulling Gabriel to his feet and steering him outside toward his car. Sergeant Laurent watched him go then turned to me with a bemused look.

'Madame, *vous avez eu beaucoup de chance*!'

'Yes, I, er, lucky, I suppose I have been.' My voice trembled. I certainly didn't feel lucky.

'Sergeant!'

Sergeant Laurent hurried outside and spoke briefly to the Inspector. As the Sergeant got into the police car, the Inspector came back inside. He looked concerned. '*Ton mari n'est pas ici?*'

'Er, no, er, Karl's not here,' I stumbled over my words feeling numb, unable to think.

The Inspector came toward me and took my arm. I allowed him to lead me toward the house.

Once inside he guided me to a seat and spoke as if to a child.
'I need to take the suspect to the station and get a statement. I will come back later to speak to you.'
I looked at the Inspector suddenly, 'Yes, it's fine, I'm fine. Don't worry.'
He didn't look convinced but merely nodded.
Once he'd gone, I roused myself to move to a more comfortable seat on the sofa. While I sat, I stared at some sort of Taschen art book on the coffee table in front of me while I tried to make sense of my ordeal. I wondered if I would ever be able to rid myself of the image of Sergeant Laurent trying to persuade Gabriel Badeau to release me. Instinctively I touched my neck where the knife had been held against it, shuddering at the memory.
A banging sound suddenly brought me to my senses as I realized someone was knocking at the door. Without focus, I stirred myself to answer it, gazing vacantly at Marie who was standing on the doorstep. She rushed forward to embrace me.
I moved to put the kettle on as if on autopilot, but Marie stopped me.
'Something stronger I think,' she said.
Pulling a bottle of wine from her shoulder bag she went to get glasses from the cupboard, glancing briefly around at the cluttered kitchen surfaces.
'I was cleaning out the cupboards' I explained with a weak smile.
She smiled cheerily and steered me toward the sofa.
'When is Karl back?'
I shook my head slowly. 'At the weekend, I think.'
She nodded.
'How did you know..?'
'The Inspector phoned me. He explained what happened and asked me to stop by to check you were coping after the shock on your own. I would have come anyway.'

I nodded and attempted a smile while Marie poured out two large glasses of wine.

'How are you here? I thought you were still in Ruffec.'

'When Geraldine got to the hospital, they ran tests and found that she was being slowly poisoned with all the drugs she'd been taking, and they couldn't find any trace of a terminal illness.'

I shook my head in disbelief at what Gabriel had done.

'I then telephoned Inspector Maupetit to tell him about the doctor, or who we thought was a doctor, and what he'd been doing to Geraldine.'

'So that's how you found out who he was?' I asked curiously.

'*Non*, the Inspector said he had recently come by some information about the man who claimed to be the doctor and that although he needed to find out more, he believed the man to be Gabriel Badeau.'

'Could that have been because of my phone call?' I wondered aloud.

'You told him the doctor was an imposter?'

'Not exactly, but I telephoned him to let him know that I'd contacted Emilie Vidale's nephew and realized as I was speaking to him, who was trying to harm Geraldine. The problem was, I didn't have a lot of time to explain in the message I left so I wasn't sure he would understand what I meant.'

Marie looked stunned. 'So you contacted him? Gabriel Badeau? You must have drawn him out, unwittingly of course, but that's why he came here. He was going to kill you too!'

I nodded. 'When I recognized his voice on the phone as that of the doctor, I panicked. I think he heard the panic and knew that I'd found him out.'

We fell silent for a few moments, thinking over the events.

'When Collette couldn't get in touch with the doctor I took Geraldine to hospital. Of course, the reason we couldn't get in touch with him must've been because he was on his way here. You might have just saved Geraldine's life but put yours in danger at the same time.'

I nodded at the irony, gazing into the middle distance.
'There was something Gabriel said which I thought rang true.'
'Oh?'
'He said if the family had been more interested in Geraldine's diagnosis and treatment they might have queried what he, as a doctor was giving her. D'you think that's the case?'
Marie shrugged, a glum look on her face. 'Geraldine wasn't exactly keen for the family to know all the details of her illness but maybe they didn't care enough to push for that information. I don't know.'
'I suppose if one or more of them had shown more interest, they might have put themselves at risk, you know, become a target for Gabriel.'
Marie nodded. 'It's good that he didn't know some of them were snooping about for the will as that could also have made him wrongly suspect they were onto him.'
'I wonder how he got away after killing Julien? I mean, there were a lot of police in the grounds. Surely someone would have spotted him.'
'*Oui*, but the doctor was known for using the garden as a short cut home. No one had any reason to suspect him even if he had been seen.'
I nodded thoughtfully and took a gulp of wine.
'He really had us all fooled didn't he?' I said ruefully.
Marie shrugged. 'Because of where he worked, he had access to medication, was able to pretend to have done tests and produce fake results. Everything looked authentic because no one was looking closely. And persuading Collette that she should be the only one to contact him when Geraldine needed help played a huge part too. I spoke to Collette before I left Ruffec and she was mortified. She blames herself that she didn't work out what he was up to.'
'But he was clever! How would she know to question a doctor's advice? And maybe it's a good job she didn't 'cos she could've been his next victim.'

Marie poured out the last drop of wine. 'Didn't I see some Cognac in among the clutter over there?'
I grinned and went to get up.
She put a hand up, 'I'll get it.'
As she traipsed across to the kitchen I checked the time. 'It's after twelve.'
'It's okay,' she called. 'I don't turn into a pumpkin.'
I chuckled.
'When did you last eat?'
'Feels like several days ago,' I grimaced.
'Okay, give me a minute,' she said as she poured out two large glasses of Cognac into tumblers, 'and I'll make us something.'
Twenty minutes later, Marie had rustled up some pasta with a cheesy sauce. 'Not the gourmet cooking you're accustomed to with Karl,' she grinned.
I smiled. 'It's delicious.'
Once we'd eaten, we sat enjoying the Cognac.
'Geraldine told me all about her affair with Victor when we in the hospital.'
'Oh really?'
'*Oui*, I think she decided she had nothing to lose. She was very weak and probably thought she would die there, but she was strong enough to talk. She confirmed that she'd told Julien he was Victor's son and said that he had inherited all his bad points.'
'From what Gabriel Badeau said, he was also Victor's son,'
Marie rolled her eyes. 'Yes, I can believe that.' She paused. 'Geraldine said that my mother was physically abused by Victor, my father, and she advised her to leave and take the children.'
'How did she know about the abuse? Did your mother tell her?'
She shook her head. 'I think Geraldine knew because they developed this close friendship and she spotted the signs.'

'So your mother left?'

She nodded. 'Geraldine told her to leave without telling Victor. She said he would have gone looking for her if he'd known where she moved to. Then one day after my mother had gone, Victor came to Geraldine's house and accused her of turning his wife against him. He became violent, demanding to know where his family had gone. Geraldine told me that he went to strike her but Henri intervened. Henri pushed Victor and he fell, hit his head and died.'

My eyebrows shot up. 'So that's how it happened!'

Marie continued, ignoring my remark. 'They placed him in the public park bordering their garden as it was easy to get at and then they left an empty bottle of whisky next to his body as well as pouring some in and around his mouth to make it look as if he'd been drinking then had fallen and hit his head. Luckily, Inspector Borné was the investigating officer and ruled it an accident. Geraldine sent my mother a letter to let her know he'd been found dead, though my mother never explained the circumstances of his death to us.'

'So Geraldine wasn't responsible for Victor's death. At least she hasn't got that on her conscience. But what about Emilie Vidale. Did she explain what happened to her?'

She nodded. 'She said she didn't know about Emilie's ill health until after Victor had caused her death, though she didn't say how he did it. Once she was dead though, he told her he would go to the police and tell them that she knew about Emilie's health problem unless she continued with her regular payments to him. She said he kept demanding more and more but she had to keep paying him even though he was the one who'd murdered Emilie. She said she thought no one would believe she was innocent.'

'And she would've lost her home.' I added.

I yawned and checked the time. It was after three.

'The bed in the spare room's already made up.'

'Great,' yawned Marie.

Marie left a note the next morning saying she had a few errands to run and wanted to see how her bread van deliveries were coping with the young girl who was acting as her stand in.
I looked around the kitchen at the mess. Time to tidy up.

CHAPTER TWENTYSIX

It was a mild sunny day so I spent some of the time wandering around the garden to check plants and trees for storm damage before using up the rest of the day cleaning the house with a renewed sense of vigour In the early evening I began looking through the information left by the *immobilier,* deciding that after my latest ordeal, moving back to the UK might not be such a bad idea after all.
I saw the Inspector approaching the house while I was gazing absently through the kitchen window and rinsing a few dishes at the sink. I opened the door before he got the chance to knock. Without any formal greeting and without even crossing the threshold, he launched into his reason for being there. His face serious.
'I wanted to let you know Madame that Genevieve was arrested and is currently being questioned.'
I nodded, unsure what to say in response. 'Oh' was all I could muster.
'You still need to make a statement though it's not urgent since Badeau has told us everything.'
I gazed at him curiously. 'I wondered…did you receive my messages? I phoned twice before, you know, everything that happened in the barn.'

He nodded. '*Mais oui,* when you mentioned the nephew in your message, I checked up on him. Of course as soon as I saw his picture I realized it was the doctor I'd interviewed. I then realized that you might have spooked him after you'd phoned him so we tried to pick him up. At the same time I received a call from Madame Reynard, er Marie, which confirmed that it was the so called doctor, Gabriel Badeau, who was the culprit. When we couldn't find him I guessed that it might be because he was coming after you so we came here instead. The rest as they say, is history.

I sighed heavily. "And it's a good job you did!" Then I heard myself say 'I'm just about to open a bottle of wine, would you like some?' His stern expression changed to one of surprise before he shrugged with a wry grin. '*D'accord.*'

I stood back to let him in and minutes later we were sitting opposite each other at the kitchen table. I moved the *immobilier* paperwork to one side before pouring our wine and noticed he couldn't help but register what it was due to the colourful brochure.

'Selling?'

I shrugged. 'Maybe.'

He nodded and looked thoughtful before speaking.

'Then what?'

'Moving back to the UK.'

He nodded; his face still serious but made no comment.

'And you?'

He gazed at me with a questioning look.

'Getting a promotion?'

'*Peut être.*'

'Then what?'

'Moving to Nantes.'

I nodded but as we met each other's gaze we struggled to suppress our amusement at how we were dancing around each other's questions.

Finally the Inspector gave in, his face transformed with a broad grin. He shook his head. '*Eh bien*, since you have been here, there's been a lot of er…' he pulled a face, struggling for the right words.
'Murders?'
He shrugged and took a sip of wine.
'My fault?' I raised my eyebrows in mock indignation.
He laughed lightly and chose his words carefully. '*La coincidence* I think.'
I smiled, grateful for the considered response.
He changed the subject. 'I was glad to hear Madame Dupont is recovering.'
'Oh, Geraldine yes, it is good news.' I paused. 'I wondered what…'
'*La maison*? What would happen about the house?' He completed my question and shook his head. 'There is no proof she knew about the owner's illness. She said that it was the *notaire* who acted without her knowledge. No one can prove otherwise.'
'And the *notaire's* death? Victor Blanchet? Will Geraldine face charges?'
He shrugged again. 'It was ruled accidental at the time so she would have to prove that it wasn't and who would want to listen to that now? The *notaire* has no living relative who is keen to dig up the past.'
I nodded, thinking of Marie and sadness swept over me.
Noting my sullen expression the Inspector suddenly held up his glass, grinning. 'A toast. To solving crime.'
I broke into a smile and gave him a knowing look. 'To fewer murders.'
He chuckled and nodded before taking a sip.
Feeling we were getting along well I said.
'I didn't realise you had a wife by the way. I didn't even know you'd been married.'
'Ex-wife,' he corrected. Getting comfortable he relaxed back into his seat and studied the wine in his glass before revealing that he'd been

divorced for two years but had only recently become friends with his ex as there'd been a lot of animosity between them during the divorce.
'Children?' I enquired.
He nodded with a smile. 'A daughter, studying in Lyon.' His expression became serious suddenly. 'That day Natalie arrived for lunch…'
I cringed at the memory of how awkward I'd felt but feigned nonchalance. Waving a dismissive hand I smiled. 'Oh please, I told you I couldn't make it and I'm not your keeper, you can dine with whomever you like. I was just disappointed because I'd heard their menu was particularly good.' I grinned.
He laughed but narrowed his eyes suspiciously. 'Okay.'
I recalled my hostility toward him on the morning I'd left Ruffec and catching his brief look of confusion I wondered if he was thinking about it too. Gazing down into my wine glass I waited awkwardly for him to take me to task over my behaviour. Fortunately he chose not to. Smiling he said, 'well, Madame…'
'Isn't it about time you called me Catherine?' I interrupted with a grin.
'Well Cat'rine,' he said slowly, focusing on his pronunciation, 'I was about to say you have a way of causing problems with my investigations.'
I giggled and interrupted. 'Are you referring to your drunken Sergeant?'
He grinned and shook his head nonplussed. 'You know he blamed you for his inebriation – as if you were pouring the wine down his throat.' He chuckled at the thought.
I giggled again. 'He was unable to resist! Once Marie sweet talked him into joining us, he succumbed to our wiles.'
The Inspector shook his head again in bewilderment but continued grinning. 'It was wrong of you, you do know that.' He gazed at me meaningfully before taking another sip, still smiling.

I give him a mock shamefaced look.

'He did look rather funny the way he wobbled away from us, but I'm hoping Lesley's cake and coffee was enough of an apology for him.'

He chuckled. 'Ah *oui*, I heard about that too.' He shook his head once again in bemusement. 'I'm very glad you are on my side.'

I gave an embarrassed laugh. 'That's nice of you to say Inspe…'

'Didier.'

'*Didier,*' I repeated, meeting his gaze.

Just then we heard a key in the lock. In surprise we both turned to find Karl letting himself in.

'Karl!' I immediately rose and went to greet him.

Karl moved to put down a large black holdall before sweeping me into his warm embrace and then staring in disbelief at the Inspector.

Sensing his confusion I began to explain that the Inspector had arrived to give me an update on a recent investigation.

'Oh?' Said Karl as he went to remove his coat, while taking in the near empty bottle of wine on the table and wine glasses. 'So what have I missed?'

He forced a smile at the Inspector who was now standing.

'I was just leaving Monsieur,' the Inspector glanced at me. 'Perhaps your wife can fill you in with the details.'

Karl gave the Inspector a direct look. 'I'm sure she will.'

There was an awkward moment of silence as the two of them stood staring at each other before the Inspector moved toward the door. I went see him out but he lifted a hand. 'Please don't bother.'

The Inspector pulled open the door while turning toward us just as Karl moved next to me, his arm encircling my waist and drawing me close.

'*Merci beaucoup* for your hospitality Madame,' said the Inspector, his face now unreadable.

Karl sighed contentedly. 'Ah, it's so good to be home.' He grinned looking from the Inspector to me. I returned his smile but had the strangest feeling that Karl's comment wasn't meant for me.
'*Bonne soirée* Monsieur,' the Inspector said now looking distinctly uncomfortable, 'Madame.' Then he was gone.

CHAPTER TWENTYSEVEN

We'd invited friends over for drinks when there was a phone call from the *immobilier*. Karl announced who the caller was before moving to take the call out of earshot of our guests. Unfortunately, everyone had already overheard him tell me who the caller was so the room hushed in anticipation of listening in.
Once the call was finished, Karl glanced around in surprise at how quiet everyone had become, before winking at me mischievously and keeping the content of the conversation to himself. When it became obvious Karl wasn't going to share any information there were a few awkward glances aimed at the two of us but gradually everyone resumed their conversations.
Around ten minutes later I was rinsing out a glass at the sink when Karl sidled up alongside.
'Someone's made an offer' He said, keeping his voice low.
I was stunned. 'Already?'
He nodded faintly. 'The interested party want to have a look round at the weekend but told the estate agent they were very keen to get things moving and would like to be moved in by Christmas.'
'What? But that gives us only two months!' I didn't know whether to laugh or cry. The estate agent had suggested we advertise the house for a price, we thought, was far too high, yet someone had offered just that.

Alerted by buzzing sound from the oven timer, Karl went to take out a tray of garlic rolls from the oven to serve with baked camembert, while I busied myself with placing some cleanly rinsed glasses onto the table. Marie and Lesley stood next to it discussing recent events.
'*Mais oui*, she was about to change her will so that Gabriel Badeau got it all.'
'But surely her children could've challenged it in the French courts.' Lesley turned to include me. 'Don't you think they would've been successful Catherine?'
I shrugged. 'Haven't a clue, but what does it matter really? Gabriel was convinced he could get everything from her. And if it had gone to court then everything would've probably come out. All the past dredged up.'
'*Oh, la la!*' Marie looked shocked. 'That would not have been good for Geraldine.'
Karl joined our group with a cheery smile, a plate of canapé's in his hand. 'Smoked salmon *tartine* anyone?'
I left Karl chatting to Marie and Lesley while I went to top up drinks, smiling suddenly at hearing Marie and Lesley burst into laughter at something Karl had said.
Di turned to me in surprise as I neared her with an open bottle of wine. 'Oh yes please.' She glanced at her companion, Monsieur Lagard. 'I was just saying that it was a good job the Inspector came out when he did.'
I shuddered. 'Oh yes, couldn't agree more.'
The *maire* looked concerned. '*Peut être* Madame Patterson would prefer not to speak of it.'
Di looked shamefaced. 'Of course! Sorry Catherine.'
'Oh don't worry about it.' I forced a cheery smile, trying not to dwell on what had happened.

Di turned back to continue her conversation as I moved away to get more wine.

'The Inspector will be missed once he takes the promotion in Nantes.' I heard her say.

"Ah I'd not heard whether he'd taken it.' Replied the *maire*.

A short while later I went to join Di and Lesley who were seated on the sofa while Karl stood nearby talking to André and Phil, Sophie and Di's respective husbands.

Overhearing André say to Karl that 'it was an amazing opportunity,' made both Di and Lesley gaze at me earnestly.

In response, and conscious of being easily overheard, Lesley lowered her voice. 'But what about *you* Catherine, what do *you* want? Come on in your heart, what do you really want to do?'

I shrugged. 'Maybe it is time to give up the sleuthing.'

'But sleuthing has been incidental hasn't it? I mean you came here to start a business,' Replied Di, her voice equally low in volume.

'Which is very successful,' added Lesley.

'There's no need to be involved in solving crimes.' Coaxed Di.

'And the Inspector certainly hasn't always been keen in your involvement. In fact, he'll probably be glad to see the back of you.' Stated Lesley matter of factly.

I stared at Lesley, grateful for her candour but at the same time, stung by her home truths.

Di glancing at Lesley with an irritated look, tried to lighten the subject. 'You have a great quality of life here Catherine.'

I was about to respond when Sophie appeared.

'You look like you're over here plotting someone's downfall!'

Sophie's smiling face was gazing down at us and I for one was glad for the interruption. Laughing lightly in response, I stood up, intending to join others with less intense dialogue.

'Ooh, comfy seat,' cooed Sophie as she took my seat on the sofa.

I moved past Karl who was now chatting to Monsieur Lagard.

'Well. going back isn't something I'd planned to do but then plans change, people change.' Karl was saying as I moved past them.

'*Oui, d'accord.*' The *maire* nodded. 'And now that Aidan's back in the UK it's easier to move back to be nearer to family, your daughter also.'

'That's right.'

'Will it be easy to arrange for somewhere to live in the small timeframe?'

'I've been looking at some newbuild houses which are not too far from where I'd be working which I know we could easily afford. It would mean my commute to work wouldn't be too cumbersome and there are plenty of shops and offices on the outskirts of the city if Catherine wanted to get a job. Though I would be earning enough for both of us.'

It was the early hours when everyone eventually left and despite their preoccupation with whether we were moving back to the UK or not, the atmosphere among our guests had been convivial.

I tossed and turned that night reminded of someone saying that happiness is simply a state of mind; be happy with what you've got rather than what you want.

I thought about the wonderful experience I'd had living in France and how maybe now was the right time to move onto a new phase in our lives. No more worrying about whether I had enough people booked into the *gîte* for the summer or whether my *chambres d'hotes* guests were happy with their rooms or whether the pool was warm enough. But then I thought about the friends I'd made, the adventures I'd had…and was filled with sadness at leaving all that behind.

What would my new life be like? I could look forward to being close to family and reacquainted with old friends. I could go out to the cinema without needing to check whether it was a *version originale*. I could enjoy a takeaway once in a while, go to the theatre or catch a train to London for an overnight stay and a west end show. There were so many things I missed about the UK but I couldn't get over the feeling that my heart would still be in France.

By morning I'd come to a decision…

Dear Reader,

I'd like you to draw your own conclusion. Does Catherine return to the UK or stay in France? If you'd like to share your thoughts, please submit a review on amazon.

Thanks for reading

GM HALEY

Printed in Great Britain
by Amazon